KV-030-894

SPECIAL MESSAGE TO READERS

THE ULVERSCROFT FOUNDATION
(registered UK charity number 264873)

was established in 1972 to provide funds for research, diagnosis and treatment of eye diseases.
Examples of major projects funded by the Ulverscroft Foundation are:-

- The Children's Eye Unit at Moorfields Eye Hospital, London
- The Ulverscroft Children's Eye Unit at Great Ormond Street Hospital for Sick Children
- Funding research into eye diseases and treatment at the Department of Ophthalmology, University of Leicester
- The Ulverscroft Vision Research Group, Institute of Child Health
- Twin operating theatres at the Western Ophthalmic Hospital, London
- The Chair of Ophthalmology at the Royal Australian College of Ophthalmologists

You can help further the work of the Foundation by making a donation or leaving a legacy.
Every contribution is gratefully received. If you would like to help support the Foundation or require further information, please contact:

THE ULVERSCROFT FOUNDATION
The Green, Bradgate Road, Anstey
Leicester LE7 7FU, England
Tel: (0116) 236 4325

website: www.foundation.ulverscroft.com

TRUSTING A STRANGER

Clara Radley's life is all about her studies until she is woken in the night by hammering on her front door. Into her world steps handsome US Special Agent Jack Henry, who tells her that her life is in danger and his job is to protect her. Henry has been sent by her biological father — a US Army General who Clara has never even met. How can she trust this stranger? But what choice does she have?

Books by Sarah Purdue
in the Linford Romance Library:

STANDING THE TEST OF TIME
PLANNING FOR LOVE
LOVE'S LANGUAGE

SARAH PURDUE

TRUSTING A STRANGER

Complete and Unabridged

LINFORD
Leicester

First published in Great Britain in 2016

First Linford Edition
published 2017

Copyright © 2016 by Sarah Purdue
All rights reserved

A catalogue record for this book is available
from the British Library.

ISBN 978–1–4448–3365–2

FLINTSHIRE SIR Y FFLINT	
C29 0000 1218 085	
ULV	£8.99

1

The hammering on the front door continued and Clara sighed, rolling onto her back. She glanced at her alarm clock, and the green glow told her it was 2:13 a.m. She threw off the pile of duvets and blankets that kept her warm in her often sub-zero student house, and used her feet to find her slippers. Forcing them on, she pulled a blanket from the bed and wrapped it round her shoulders — looking, she knew, like a refugee. She allowed the irritation inside to well up. This time, her housemates had gone too far, and she was going to tell them exactly what she thought.

She fumbled for the light switch in the hall, turned it on, and squinted in the brightness. More by feel than sight, she made her way down the steep staircase to the front door. She had tried to ignore the housemate outside, hoping he or she would give up and go away, but no luck. She couldn't sleep through all the racket, so had decided to get up, let them in, and then yell at them until they begged for forgiveness. In their moment of weakness, she might even be able to get a promise that they would wash up the week-old dishes in the kitchen sink. Being a postgrad was not easy. You were still a student, but you were too old to live like one!

Clara gave the front door the sharp pull it required to open, since it would swell in the winter, opened her mouth to begin the lecture she had been mentally preparing — and stopped. Her sleepy brain fought to make sense of what it saw: drunken housemates she had been expecting; but a man and two women in suits, not so much.

'Miss Radley?' one of the female suits asked.

'Er . . . ' was about all Clara could manage.

'Miss *Clara* Radley?'

'Yes,' Clara answered, forcing some

composure into her voice and racking her brains for reasons why three smartly dressed strangers might be knocking on her door in the middle of the night. She had a dim image of door-to-door salesmen, but pushed it aside.

'I'm DI Cathy Jacobs, Metropolitan Police.' She flashed a badge in a black leather holder in front of Clara's eyes, but it was so fast that Clara had no idea if it was a police ID or a bus pass.

'This is my colleague, DS Lyn Hanson. Can we come in, please?'

A sense of foreboding threatened to overwhelm Clara. Police in the middle of the night could surely mean only one thing — someone had died. She stood back from the door and directed the inspector into the front room. The two female officers walked past and perched on the tatty sofa that ran under the front window.

The man on the doorstep didn't move, and Clara felt embarrassed for him that the women had not felt the need to introduce him. He, on the other hand, did not seem remotely bothered. She looked at him closely for the first time. He was dressed in a sharp black suit that fitted him well, with a sombre tie that at first glance also appeared a conservative black, though as the light from the streetlamps caught it, Clara could make out an embossed pattern of stars and stripes. His hair was dark brown and closely cropped to his head; shorter, in Clara's opinion, than was strictly fashionable. Despite the cut of the suit, and how well it fitted, Clara couldn't help but feel that he would be more comfortable wearing something else.

She mentally shook herself; clearly she was in shock. She wouldn't normally gape at strange men standing on her doorstep like some kind of goldfish. 'Sorry,' she said, despite the fact that she knew she had nothing to apologise for. 'Please come in.'

The man nodded.

'Thank you, ma'am.' His accent was distinctive and American.

He brushed past her in the narrow hall and Clara felt a jolt. He was so close that she could smell his after-shave, sharp and musky. She took a breath before closing the door and forcing herself to focus. Something was wrong, terribly wrong, and she needed to find out what.

She made herself walk into the lounge and sit in her favourite arm-chair. The two police officers wore carefully neutral expressions. 'Please tell me what's happened,' she blurted out, feeling fear rising up from deep inside her. 'I know something must be wrong. Has somebody died? I don't normally have visitors at this time of night.' She knew she was babbling like a fool, but she didn't care. She was terrified of what they were going to say; but, like taking off a sticking plaster, she needed to get it over with.

'No one's died, Miss Radley.' It was the suited man who spoke and not the police officers. Clara swivelled her head to look at him. 'I need to speak with you about your father.'

'Jason?' Clara said. The two police officers exchanged glances

'No, ma'am,' the man said. She wished he would stop calling her 'ma'am'. 'The matter is not regarding your stepfather, Jason Radley, but your biological father, George Driscoll.'

The man waited patiently while Clara assimilated this information. Briefly, she wondered if she was dreaming. Why on earth would a handsome American man — because, despite the shock, she couldn't help but register that he *was* extremely handsome — be coming to see her in the middle of the night to talk about George? She allowed herself a small smile. Yep, she was definitely dreaming. She looked up again, saw that all three visitors were regarding her with a level of concern, and felt suddenly sure that they all thought she was crazy.

'I'm sorry,' Clara said, 'but I don't understand.' This seemed like the best response, as she really did have no idea.

'Your father is George Driscoll, General George Driscoll of the United States Army,' the man said, making a statement rather than asking a question.

'So I've been led to believe,' Clara said, looking the handsome man full in the face. He merely raised an eyebrow. She found a patch of bare skin on her arm and gave it a firm pinch. That was supposed to be the way to wake you up from a dream, wasn't it? But no luck. She was still sitting in her front room in the middle of the night with a strange, but easy-on-the-eye, American man, and two female police officers who so far had made no contribution to the story.

Clara looked him in the eye and expanded on her statement. 'I've never met him — George, that is. He and my mum had a brief fling while she was studying at Columbia University, and I was the result. She came home and had me, then met Jason, my stepfather. Jason's my dad; or at least the only dad I really have.'

Clara frowned. She couldn't believe

she was talking to strangers about this. It was so personal and private. Hardly any of her friends, even, knew that Jason wasn't her biological father. He had adopted her when she was four, and she had always called him 'Dad'. 'So I'm sorry, but I still don't understand,' she said, before lifting a hand to smooth down her bed-hair. She probably looked in a right state.

'My name is Jackson Henry, Miss Radley, and your father sent me to speak with you. I'm a federal agent working for Army intelligence.'

Clara barked out a laugh. This was getting more and more ridiculous, and she had an ominous feeling that she was either going to appear on some reality TV show as a prize class idiot, or that she had been daft enough to let three strangers into her house — when she was alone — who had goodness knew what planned for her.

She stood up. 'I'm not sure what kind of joke you think you're playing, or how you found out about my biological father, but I think you should leave. I've heard enough.' She held out one arm in the direction of the front door, as if this would be enough to get them to leave.

'I'm afraid I can't do that, Miss Radley,' Jackson Henry said.

'Then I'll call the police,' Clara said, before frowning. She wasn't sure how that worked when the police already seemed to be there. She turned her attention to the DI who had first introduced herself. 'I would like you to leave now,' Clara said, addressing her comment to the detective inspector.

To her credit, the DI looked most uncomfortable. 'I'm afraid Agent Henry is right, Miss Radley. We do need to speak with you about your biological father.' The DI said the word 'father' carefully, as if she at least was aware of how Clara must feel about the man she had never met. 'I'm a detective inspector in the Close Protection Squad,' she continued, as if by way of explanation.

Clara frowned. 'Isn't that for the government and royal family?' None of this made any sense, and she could feel herself getting irritated.

'Yes. We provide protection for high-profile individuals and their families the royals, members of the cabinet, and also the military and security services.'

'Right,' Clara said. 'But none of my family fit into any of those categories.'

'Your father does, and therefore so do you,' Jackson said.

'My father, as you call him, has never once been in touch. Not a birthday card, not even a phone call. I could walk past him on the street and not realise. I don't even know what he looks like.' Clara could feel herself blush. That last part wasn't strictly true; she had googled General George Driscoll, and knew exactly what he looked like.

'Nevertheless,' Jackson continued, his accent starting to annoy Clara, 'the news of your relationship has become public in the US, and raises a significant risk.'

Clara laughed. 'From who?'

His face was a mask of seriousness. 'Enemies both foreign and domestic.'

He sounded so much like a politician giving a speech that Clara nearly laughed. She looked at the two policewomen, hoping to detect signs that they were in on what was clearly a joke, but both the faces that looked back wore solemn expressions. Clara was beginning to feel panic pricking at the edge of her brain. If this was real, if this was really happening, what did it mean?

'We have some information, Miss Radley,' Jackson answered. 'Some information that we believe is a credible threat.'

'Against George?' Clara said. 'I would imagine he can look after himself; he *is* a Marine!' She knew she had failed to keep the mocking tone from her voice, and watched as Jackson bristled slightly, seemingly unable to completely hide his feelings.

'General Driscoll has security, and is able to assess any threats to his person and take action.' His tone was neutral and the professional mask was firmly back in place.

'So you came all the way from the United States to tell me that the father I've never even met has had threats made against him?' She was incredulous now.

'No, ma'am, I came all the way from the United States to tell you that there have been credible threats made against you.'

2

Jackson watched as Clara felt for the chair behind her and sat down heavily. He kept his face neutral, not allowing his concern to show. What Clara needed right now was calm professionalism, and that was what he was good at. The General had shown him a photograph of her during his briefing, but it did not do her justice. Even now, in a moment of shock and fear, she had a radiance to her. She was tall and willowy, which she must get from her mother, since the General was broad and not particularly tall; yet there was something about her that said she was Driscoll's daughter.

'Me?' was all Clara could manage.

Jackson forced his mind back to business. 'Miss Radley, I know this has come as a great shock to you, but unfortunately we don't have time to go into the details right now. We need to leave. Immediately.'

'I'm sorry, what? Leave? I can't leave; it's mid-term.'

Jackson moved towards her chair. He seemed taller now than he had when he'd stood on her front doorstep. She could almost feel the crick in her neck starting to niggle as she had to look upwards. He noted her discomfort and knelt beside the chair, reaching out and placing his hand on her arm.

'We have to leave — tonight, now. The risk is real, Miss Radley.'

Clara shook her head. 'So I need to go home? I have so much to work to do, but I suppose I could take most of it with me . . . ' Her mind raced ahead, trying to work out how best she could study back at home with her parents.

'No,' Jackson said, and she looked at him sharply. 'You can't go to your mother's. If you do, you'll put her and the rest of your family in danger.'

Clara stared at him. She felt like she was in some kind of bad movie. 'You're being ridiculous!' she said, shaking off

14

his hand. 'What would anyone want with me or my family? We aren't important — we're just average people!' She had been afraid before, for herself, but she could live with that. But putting her mum, Jason, and the kids in danger — that was a terrible thing to say!

'You could be used against your father, if the wrong people got hold of you.'

Clara stood again and crossed the room. She needed to put some distance between herself and this man. She couldn't think straight with him so close to her. 'My father doesn't even know me! What is it to him if something happens to me? Surely all you need to do is tell the press that we have no relationship, and then they'll leave us alone.'

Jackson shook his head. 'It doesn't work like that.' He wanted to explain the level of danger she was in. He was sure now, from this brief meeting, that she could handle it — but they didn't have time.

'Are you worried about his reputation? Worried what the public will think when they find out he has a daughter he's never even met?' Clara's voice was raised now, and she knew she was shouting at the wrong person. She should save her anger for her supposed father, if she ever got the chance to tell him what she thought of him.

'This has nothing to do with his reputation, which is solid, and something you should be proud of.' Jackson took a visible breath to quell his temper. 'This is all about your safety, Miss Radley. Whilst your father has never been able to play an active role in your life . . . ' Clara snorted, but Jackson continued, undeterred. ' . . . he cares for you and your mother.'

Clara shook her head, but held her tongue. There was clearly no point in arguing with this man, who seemed to be blindly devoted to her father.

'The fact remains that you're all in danger. If you won't believe that about yourself, then please at least consider

16

your family.' Jackson held Clara's stare, knowing that he was being unfair, but that right now he needed to say something to galvanise her into action. He watched as a flicker of fear passed over her face, quickly replaced with indignation.

She glared at him. How dare this man, who knew nothing about her, suggest that she would ever willingly put her family in danger? 'How?' she asked.

'Come again?'

'How are they in danger? I mean, I suppose I can see why I might be, but not why they would be.'

'They could be used to get at you.'

Those words sent a coldness straight through Clara that settled in her heart. She thought for a moment that it had ceased beating, and she could feel herself start to shake.

Jackson reached out to steady her, wondering if his assessment of her inner strength was off and that she was going to faint. It would make it easier if he could simply carry her to the car; but part of him wanted her to fight it, to be the General's daughter in spirit. He watched carefully as she forced her body to obey her, to get a grip.

Taking a deep breath, she said, 'How do I keep them safe?' She looked him in the eye, wanting to check that his answer was the truth.

'Right now, the best thing you can do for them is to leave. DI Jacobs and DS Hanson will provide security for us to the airport. You need to get dressed, but there's no time to gather belongings. We can get you anything you need on the way.'

'On the way where?'

'Washington, ma'am.'

'America? I can't go to the States! I don't even have my passport, it's at home!'

'We have all that covered, Miss Radley. Please, we've wasted enough time. Go and put some clothes on.'

Clara headed to the door, feeling overwhelmed with information she couldn't process. 'Wait — I don't think the kids even have passports. Have you got spares for them too?'

Jackson shook his head. 'They'll be staying in Britain under the care of the Close Protection Squad. The risk to them will be greatly reduced once it becomes known that you're no longer in the country.'

Clara's desire to keep her family safe, even if this all turned out to be some kind of hoax, conflicted with her desire to be with the people she cared most about in this world. She turned to speak again, but Jackson was on his phone, and the two officers were discussing lead cars and routes to the airport. Clara shook her head again in confusion. This was so far-fetched and crazy! It had to be some kind of mistake. But one thing she knew: she would not take even the smallest risk with the safety of her mum, Jason, and her brothers. She'd go along with it for now and just hope that the whole mess got sorted out soon.

She went to her room, where she pulled on her jeans and tried to decide what else to wear. She pulled open a drawer and looked at the different jumpers and shirts. Glancing at her bedside table, she saw her mobile phone, where she had left it when she went to bed. In a split second she had made up her mind. She would call her mum. If she could just hear her voice, and be reassured that they were all fine; feel reassured herself, and maybe even ask her mum if this could possibly be true . . .

As she reached out for her phone, the bedroom door swung open. Jackson had made his way quietly upstairs. She let out a small scream and then grabbed a pillow from her bed to cover her top half. 'What do you think you're doing?' she yelled, more loudly than was strictly necessary. 'I'm getting dressed in here!'

'Give me the cell phone, Miss Radley,' Jackson said, holding out his hand, glad he had trusted his instinct that she might try to contact her family.

He understood her reasons, but it was too dangerous.

'No — you can't tell me what to do. I'm not a child! I'm twenty-five years old, for goodness' sake! I'm going to phone my mum, just to check in and make sure everything's OK with them.' Even as she said it, Clara realised that she sounded childish.

'Give me the phone.' Jackson had set his tone to 'command', and Clara knew it. She briefly wondered about refusing, but suspected that it might end in a scuffle. At any other time, a scuffle with this man might be appealing, but not now. Carefully holding the pillow in place, she handed the phone over.

'Do I get it back later?'

He studied her face. 'Maybe, depending on how the extraction goes. You have twenty seconds to finishing getting dressed, then we're leaving.'

He strode from the room. Clara poked out her tongue at his retreating back, and she wasn't embarrassed to think that it made her feel marginally better. She pulled a white shirt from the open drawer and shrugged into it before grabbing her oldest but most-loved jumper. She looked around her room and tried not think about all the things that she should be taking with her. As she heard footsteps on the stairs, she reached out to a drawer, pulling out a photo of herself with her family last Christmas and shoving it in her pocket, just as the door sprung open and Jackson grabbed her arm.

'We have to go.' This time it was definitely a command, and action followed. He pulled her out of the room and down the stairs so fast that her feet barely kept her upright. The front door was open and she could see three cars with no markings parked at angles to the kerb. Hardly inconspicuous in an area of small terraced houses with ten-year-old wrecks parked outside.

Jackson looked left and right, keeping Clara behind him and protected. The middle car had an open back door, and he swung her in front of him and shoved her into the back in one swift movement. He was thankful that she had the sense to duck and therefore saved herself from a crack to the head. He yanked the door closed behind him.

'Move, move,' he yelled; and with a squeal of tyres that Clara felt sure would wake the neighbours, they raced off into the night.

She struggled to sit upright. Once she was, she felt Jackson reach across her for the seatbelt. Pulling it sharply, he rammed it home with a click. He pointed to a small button on the belt across her chest and lifted her left hand up to hold it.

'If I say 'down', get your head down, and when we've stopped, press this.' She must have looked confused because he added, 'It's an emergency release.'

He turned his head from her, and for the first time she could see his small plastic earpiece. By watching his face, she could tell he was listening intently to whoever was speaking.

'Route tango,' he said out loud. The

23

car braked suddenly and took a small side road off the main road, weaving in and out of the cars parked on the residential street. Within minutes they were on a country lane. Clara looked out of the window, trying to get her bearings, but there were no street lights in this part of York; and the driver of the car, who she could not see, clicked off the headlights. They were driving blind.

Clara's hand clenched the door handle, but this was not enough to keep her steady in the swiftly moving vehicle. The car took a ninety-degree left-hand turn and she was thrown sideways, the seat belt tightening painfully across her chest and neck while her head jerked. Jackson shifted beside her, reached out and took her hand. She wasn't sure if it was for reassurance or so he could drag her from the car quickly if it stopped, but she was glad of it in the darkness.

'He has night-vision goggles on,' he said, feeling her shake with fear. 'He can see just fine.'

Clara let out her held-in breath and

tried to force herself to calm down. There was a dazzling flash of headlights ahead. She let go of the door handle and tried to shield her eyes. The car veered right and then left as if it had hit a patch of slick mud. Jackson seemed unaffected by the rapid changes and sat as still as if they were driving ten miles an hour in a straight line.

There was a sound of squealing tyres so loud that Clara thought it would overwhelm her, and then the shockwave hit, throwing her back into her seat, her head bumping painfully against the window to her right. The car lurched again, and then she felt she was falling, the world spinning, and she hoped against hope she was about to wake up from the dream that had turned into a nightmare.

There were stars dancing in front of her eyes, and she tried to work out where she was and what had happened. Her head was pounding and her left eye felt swollen. Something was tight across her chest, and then it was suddenly released and she was thrown forward. She felt a sharp pain in her right arm, but before she could do anything, someone was pulling at her. She tried to resist, tried to work out what was happening. The eerie stillness was punctuated by popping sounds. Her jumper snagged on something and she tried to turn and release it, but her left hand was held tightly and she could not seem to make her right hand work. The arms kept pulling, and she felt and heard the jumper rip.

'Keep quiet,' a voice said harshly in her ear, so close that she could feel the breath on her skin. She felt the ground beneath her feet and then she was being dragged along, away from where she had been; but by whom, she couldn't tell.

3

Clara fought to get her bearings. They were running towards the pitch darkness and away from the small amount of light that spilled from the headlights of the other car. She could hear muffled voices and a *pop, pop* noise, which she couldn't place but seemed ominous. The hand in hers gripped tightly but gave no clue as to the identity of its owner, and so Clara had no idea if she was running away from the danger or straight into it. Her mind still fought to make sense of it all. Five hours ago she had been tucked up in bed, and the only thing she had to worry about was what she was going to tell her doctorate supervisor about her lack of progress. Now she was fleeing for her life because of a man who happened to be her father, but whom she had never met.

The anger flared again. His only

contribution to her existence since conception was this mess. He had put her life and those of her family in danger, and she had had enough. Without a word of warning she forced her legs to stop moving; not easy with the adrenaline coursing through her and her natural instinct to run. But the hand in hers pulled her forward.

'We have to keep moving.' The voice came as a harsh whisper, but Clara recognised it as belonging to Jackson, so at least she now knew who she was running with — the man her father had sent to keep her safe. Or had he? She had no way of knowing if anything she'd been told was true, or if General George Driscoll knew anything about it. What if she was with the very man the General was trying to protect her from? She dug in her heels, and despite the tugging she managed to stay upright and still. One thing was for sure: she wasn't moving until she had some answers.

'Who are you really?' she demanded,

breathless from the run. She could barely make out that he had turned his head towards her in the moonlight.

'I told you. Special Agent Jackson Henry, US Army Intelligence. Your father sent me to retrieve you. Now move!'

It was the terse voice of a soldier, but Clara wasn't having any of it. 'Where are the two detectives, the ones from Close Protection?'

She could feel the frustration flowing from the man standing opposite her. 'I don't know, Clara. I didn't stay to find out. My mission is to keep you safe, and I intend to.'

'But how do I know that what you are saying is the truth? She could feel her voice shake, and forced herself to stay calm.

'We're in the middle of a forest being pursued by some unpleasant people who, let's just say, do not have your best interests at heart. What other kind of proof do you think I can offer you right now?'

Clara racked her brains for something that would give her a sign that her instinct was right. She felt deep down that she could trust this man, but had no idea where this was coming from. She wondered if it was because he was handsome and a sort of hero type — the type she had secretly always wanted to be rescued by as a teenager. But she wasn't a child anymore, and this wasn't a fantasy — this was real.

'How do I know I can trust you?' she asked, though she knew it was a foolish question. What was she expecting him to say?

'Trust me, or wait for the others to catch up and take your chances with them. What'll it be?'

His voice was quiet, but there was no mistaking the urgency. Clara knew it wasn't a choice at all. She had to trust him; there was no one else. The people behind had run them off the road with no thought for her safety. Whatever danger lay ahead with Jackson Henry, it was likely to be less than what lay behind. She said nothing, but took a step forward, and without a word they were running again into the blackness.

Clara's breath was ragged. She forced the cold air in and out of her lungs and tried to ignore the burning pain. She had lost all sense of time and had no idea how long they had been running, or where they were running to. She just hoped that Jackson had some sort of plan. They had rested for a few seconds, but a noise behind them had sent them hurtling forward. Clara wasn't sure how much longer she could keep going. Her head and arm throbbed, and she tried again to push away the pain; to focus on what was important right now, in this moment. But with the pain also came nausea, which she was barely keeping in check. The fear of being pursued threatened to overwhelm her, and she had an urge to just shout out and get it over with; just like when she was a child and playing hide-and-seek, when she would tell the seeker where she was rather than wait to be found.

'Stop . . . I need to stop.' Her voice came out in short gasps,

The tension on her hand reduced and their pace slowed. She was guided to a tall tree, and a hand on her shoulder gently pushed her down so that she was sitting against it. She pulled her jumper up over her nose and tried to slow her breathing. Through the jumper the air warmed, and the pain in her lungs lessened. She cradled her right arm in her left, feeling certain that it was broken. She felt Jackson crouch down beside her. He didn't seem to be out of breath, and she tried to decide if she was annoyed or impressed. Under the circumstances, she went for annoyed; this was no time to get gooey-eyed.

'Another couple of miles and we'll be at a safe place to stop,' he said quietly, all the time surveying the woods around them. 'Then I'll take a look at your arm and your head.'

She nodded, unable to speak. He stood and moved a few paces away from her, scanning their surroundings for things that she did not want to think about.

'How do you know where we are? We could be anywhere,' Clara said.

'I memorised the route and the escape points. We're heading towards a disused farm building that we had pegged as an RVP.'

'RVP?'

'Rendezvous point. There'll be a secure phone left there so we can contact base and be on our way again.'

Clara marvelled at his calmness, but she had met individuals like him before. She'd spent some time abroad working, mainly in Africa, for a charity. Some of her colleagues there had been ex-military and had provided much-needed security. Jackson was either in the military or had been, that much she was certain of.

Her breathing had barely slowed before she was being hauled to her feet again. Reluctantly, she forced her feet to start moving. They stopped again, and Clara waited as Jackson seemed to be checking the area. Apparently satisfied, he pulled her to the left and, holding back some dense bracken, he gestured for her to hide. When she was settled, he let the bracken fall back into place. As he turned to leave, she reached out her working left hand for his arm, feeling the panic well up inside her.

'You're not leaving me here?'

'I need to check it's safe. I'll be back.'

Despite his words, Clara couldn't make herself let go. She felt a hand on her cheek and found herself leaning into it.

'You're safe here, and I promise I'll come back for you.'

Clara wished she could see his eyes, the best way to know if he was telling the truth, but all she could make out was the shadow of his head. She nodded, not knowing whether he could see the gesture in the darkness, and gently he lifted her hand from his arm.

Clara waited, her heart thudding in her chest, and made herself count backwards from a hundred. She had to focus on something other than being alone in the middle of nowhere with

34

people who wanted to hurt her on her trail. She reached the number one, and Jackson was still not back. Refusing to give in to the fear, she started again, but this time from one thousand. She was shaking with cold and fear, and each jarring movement sent new waves of pain through her body. She needed to lie down, to feel safe and to be safe.

At seven hundred and eight, she felt movement to her right. She froze and stopped mouthing the numbers to herself, holding her breath with her eyes closed. Seeing shadows was worse than seeing danger in broad daylight. Again she had the overwhelming urge to stop the feelings inside her; to announce her presence and just get it over with.

'Clara?' a voice whispered.

She fought down a scream and launched herself out of the bracken in the direction of the voice. Arms caught her before she fell to the ground, and she could feel herself pulled tightly into a hug.

It was important to keep her calm,

Jackson told himself, and to make her feel safe; to get her to trust him. He wouldn't let himself be distracted by the fact that he had wanted to pull her into his arms the first moment he saw her.

'It's me,' he said. 'Stay low and quiet.'

The arms released her, and for a moment Clara wobbled and wondered if she had finally hit the wall; that her body was going to give up on her. But somehow, through gritted teeth, she forced herself to stay upright. His hand in hers, she followed him, marvelling at how quietly he could move. They left the shadowy canopy of trees, and ahead she could just make out the wreck of a building in the moonlight. It looked to be made of wood and plastic sheeting. The weight of the roof had shifted the walls sideways so that it had a drunken appearance. Clara did not think she had ever been so glad to see something in her life.

They crept forward and Jackson

shifted a panel of wall, holding it up so that Clara could step through. She walked forward a few paces but could see little in the gloom. She felt Jackson step in behind her.

'No lights, I'm afraid, but we have water and some blankets. The cavalry will be here in an hour.'

He lifted an old seed sack and pulled out a bottle of water. He handed it to Clara and she drank greedily, water spilling down her chin. Self-consciously, she wiped it away.

'Then what?' She had been so focused on getting away from the men in the car that she had not considered what their next move would be.

'We get you to the airport and onto a plane. Once we're on home soil, it'll be easier to keep you safe.'

Clara frowned, wondering if that was supposed to be a negative comment about England, but decided she was too tired to care. Jackson seem oblivious to any insult and handed her blanket.

'Here, you look cold. Wrap yourself

in this. Cover your head, too; that's where you lose the most heat.'

She rolled her eyes. Did Jackson think she was a child? Then she answered her own question — of course he did. Just as a parent will always see the child in the grown-up that stands before them, so Jackson would only ever see General Driscoll's helpless little girl. She didn't know why this thought seemed to bother her. She winced as something wet was pressed to her forehead.

'You've a nasty contusion, but the bleeding's stopped. You're going to have quite a headache tomorrow.' He couldn't help but admire her. Many a stronger person would be a quivering wreck right now. Her inner strength was at odds with her fragile outward appearance. Again he was reminded of her father, and again he forced back the thoughts and feelings that threatened to get in the way of the job that he had to do.

Clara couldn't help shuddering at the thought of tomorrow. Her head was already pounding, and any movement of her neck sent sharp stabs of pain behind her eyes. She only hoped that by tomorrow she would be in the vicinity of some aspirin.

Jackson reached gently for her right hand, and, watching his face, she could see it crease momentarily in sympathy. 'Looks broken to me. I'll strap it up as best I can and get you to a doctor as soon as possible.'

She watched as he deftly supported each side of her wrist with pieces of wood he had found on the floor, no doubt once part of the dilapidated building. Using his tie, he firmly bandaged her arm to the new support. She had been expecting more pain, but it seemed to lessen, and she smiled at him gratefully. For a brief second he smiled back, then seemed to remember himself. He turned away.

'Get some sleep,' he said before moving away from her to check outside.

Clara took the blanket and wrapped it around herself before looking for a suitable spot. There didn't seem to be one, so she simply lay down. With her mind whirring and the pain from her injuries, she doubted she would be able to sleep; but within minutes, tiredness swamped her and she drifted off.

A noise woke her, loud and throbbing. Light seemed to spill into the broken-down shed from every conceivable angle. She tried to work out where she was and what was happening, trying to sort the jumble of memories and dreams into any sense of order.

She put her arms out in order to fumble her way to her knees, and was rewarded with a shot of pain that started in her hand and made its way to the top of her head. A wave of dizziness swept over her, and it seemed as if the floor was moving up towards her fast. Then she felt arms scoop her up.

She struggled to find her feet, trying to get away, but the arms held her tightly. She could feel breath on her ear and she knew someone was trying to speak, but she could hear nothing that her brain could process into words.

Outside there was more light, and a sharp wind that made her hair dance. She turned her face away from it and clutched tightly to whoever was holding her. The noise, the fear and the pain were too much, and she felt the pull of the darkness. She gave in, slipping away from the world around her.

4

The first thing that Clara became aware of was a humming noise so loud that it made her teeth vibrate. She tried to open her eyes, but only one would co-operate; the other seemed as if it had been glued shut. Searching her disjointed memories, she recalled her head bumping against a car window, and suddenly the swollen eye made sense. All at once, the fractured images fell into place, and the events of the night became clear. She tried to sit up and found that she couldn't; a belt around her feet and one about her middle kept in her place.

Looking around with her one good eye, she made out what seemed to be the inside of an airplane — but not a commercial jet. It was more like a military cargo plane. She was wrapped in heavy blankets, and an IV line ran into her uninjured hand. The other arm was in an inflatable cast, and the lack of pain told her that she was being well looked after.

A figure in green fatigues and a heavy-looking headset approached with a friendly smile. Clara tentatively smiled back, hoping that she was safe; that she was with Jackson. She scanned the rest of the interior, but could see no sign of him and frowned. The figure in green fatigues gently placed a headset onto her head and adjusted the microphone so that it sat in front of her mouth.

'Miss Radley, I'm Lieutenant Birmingham.' The voice was female and pitched softly, despite the background noise. It was the drawl of an American, and from Clara's limited knowledge she would have said from somewhere in the south.

'You're quite safe with us, ma'am. I know that you've had quite a time of it, but you're on board a US Air Force plane bound for Andrews Airbase near

Washington DC. We'll be landing in about three hours.'

Clara smiled — it had been a succinct report covering all of her questions, bar one. Where was Jackson? Had he completed his task and now abandoned her? She forced the thought from her mind. Right now, any familiar face would have been welcome.

'Do you have any pain, ma'am?' The voice came over Clara's headset and she shook her head. She wasn't in pain — they seemed to have taken care of that — but she felt horribly alone, despite the kindness of the lieutenant.

'Can I get you anything? Something to drink or eat?'

Clara shook her head again. She didn't think she could eat and certainly wasn't hungry.

'I'll go tell Agent Henry you're awake.'

Clara felt relief wash over her and wondered if the lieutenant could read minds. She had known the man for less than a day, but she wanted so desperately to see him. She knew that when she did, the fear would recede and she would feel safe.

She watched Birmingham move carefully down the cabin and then hammer on the door which Clara imagined led to the cockpit. It was pulled open — Clara couldn't see by whom — and then she could see the lieutenant's mouth moving but couldn't hear the words, guessing that her own headset didn't link her to the rest of the plane. Birmingham stepped to the side, and a man who was tall and broad, dressed in similar green combats with a heavy helmet, stepped out before Birmingham disappeared into the cockpit. Clara's eyes followed the figure as he found a perch on the bench opposite.

'How are you feeling?' the voice said; and despite the distortion and the overwhelming whine of engines, she knew that it was Jackson. She managed a smile.

'Not bad, thanks to you.' She felt

embarrassed to say it, but needed to express her gratitude.

'You did pretty well yourself. That wasn't easy terrain with a broken arm and a head injury.'

Clara could feel a glow inside her and hoped feverishly that it wouldn't make its way to her face. 'Are you all right?' she asked; studying his face, she could see him raise an eyebrow.

'Just another day at the office,' he said with a grin.

Clara tried to imagine what life would be like if every day for him was like this one. He seemed to thrive off the adrenaline and the fear, but she wasn't sure that she would ever want another day like that again. She wasn't sure what to say, and as Jackson seemed content to let her be, she let her mind drift. Something had been nagging at her — something she wanted to ask; that she needed to know. She allowed herself to examine recent events, and then it was there. The thought jolted her and she tried to sit up.

'Easy, Miss Radley. What's wrong?' There was unmistakable concern in his voice; although whether he was just doing his duty, or genuinely cared, she wasn't certain.

'My family,' she blurted out, and tried to fight the images of them in trouble, being hurt, that had suddenly appeared in her mind. She felt a hand rest on her should and push her back gently.

'They're safe, as promised. The Close Protection Squad have them at a safe house and will reassess the threat level when we're wheels down.'

Clara tried to study his face — which was difficult with the helmet, fixed sunglasses and microphone — as she searched for the truth. She relaxed back into the pillows and hoped against hope that they were indeed safe. 'When will I be able to speak to them?' she asked, mindful that she no longer had her mobile, and trying to remember what the international code was to ring home. She knew that she would try, the first chance she got, whether her 'father' approved of it or not.

'Like I said, we'll review things once we're safely at home plate.'

Clara knew she had to be content with this, and suspected it was not his call anyway. He was focused on his task, to transport her safely to America and her father.

' 'We' meaning General Driscoll?'

The now-familiar raised eyebrow was back. Jackson wanted to smile but forced his face to neutral. He liked this woman; she had a fire to her. She was more like the General than she could know, and he wondered how their first meeting would go. There was clearly a lot of resentment and hurt hidden beneath the surface.

'The General will be the one to decide,' he answered simply, knowing that this would probably make her angry. But it was, after all, the truth.

'Do I even have a say?' she asked, not bothering to hide her rising anger.

'You'll need to speak with the

General about that.'

It was clear to Jackson that his acceptance of the General's apparent absolute right to decide everything irritated her to the point that she could not think of any response. Her face was like an open book, and he could read it clearly. He knew that to her, it must seem like he didn't have a mind of his own. She was probably wondering if he was just another soldier who blindly obeyed orders no matter what the consequences. If she did think that, it was probably for the best.

'I'm sure you'll feel better after some sleep and a hot meal,' he said, and Clara felt at once like a toddler being pacified. She gave him one of her looks, but she was fairly sure it was lost on him due to her swollen face, and in fact it sent a dull ache through to her teeth. She hated to admit it, but he was right; she was going to need a clear head when they landed. She was going to have to deal with her errant father and find a way to get back home to her real family, and to do that she needed to be sharp.

'You're right,' she said abruptly, 'I need to sleep.' She wondered if she had sounded rude and then wondered why she cared. Everything was so mixed up, and she didn't know how she felt about any of it. Turning her face away from him, she shut her eyes and willed herself to let go and sleep. She didn't turn back, but she could feel his eyes watching her and so kept her face smooth. She didn't want to talk to him right now; she had nothing to say, and he had nothing to give her that would help her get home.

The three hours took forever to pass, particularly since Clara was faking sleep. With her eyes closed, she tried to work out what she was going to do and what she was going to say to the General. She'd decided on one thing, though: at no point was she going to call him 'Dad'. That was a title that you earned by being present in your child's life, and the General in no way qualified for it. He had made himself a stranger to her; had made his choice. So 'General' it was.

She felt the air pressure shift and decided that she had been faking sleep long enough. She turned her head and did her best impression of someone who had woken from a deep sleep.

'We're cleared for landing. It might be a bit rougher than you're used to,' Jackson said, seeing that she had her eyes open. Clara marvelled at how he had made yet another assumption about her, but really that was no surprise. If everything he knew about her was from the General, who knew nothing about her, then what did she expect?

'Try landing in an eight-person plane in southern Somalia on what passes for a runway.' She knew she was boasting but she couldn't help it. She wanted to prove that she was more than he thought, but also she wanted to share part of herself with him.

'Somalia?' he said, having the good grace to sound surprised. Jackson knew there was more to this woman than met the eye. He knew, of course, that she had travelled and worked abroad, but there had been no time for a detailed briefing before he'd made his mercy dash.

'I spent two years with Medicine for Africa. We landed in some pretty rough areas.' Clara tried to sound nonchalant but was sure she wasn't pulling it off.

'I can imagine.' Jackson cocked his head to one side. 'This should be no problem for you, then.' And as if by instinct, he reached up and grabbed a thick strap suspended from the ceiling just as the plane banked sharply to the right. Clara let out a high-pitched scream, which she was sure he couldn't hear but was equally sure that he could see. A hand reached out for her shoulder; part of her wanted to shrug it off, and the other part wanted it to wrap her into a tight hug.

The airplane banked again and the air pressure changed once more as they made a rapid descent. With a scream of engines and a heavy thud, they were down. Clara let out her held-in breath. Somalia had been worse, she told herself sternly. This was nothing. There were no windows to look out of, so she couldn't tell if it was day or night or even where they were. The side door was opened by a member of the crew, and Clara could hear the sound of machinery and more American voices. She had never been to America, and she supposed that this was one way to arrange a visit.

Men and women in Air Force and Army uniforms seemed to swarm over the plane. Then the stretcher that Clara was lying on was lifted up and she was outside. The breeze was cool and the light seemed to be fading — or was it dawn? Clara had no idea which. She tried to recall the time difference, but her mind was fuzzy and refused to focus. She was unloaded from the airplane and into the back of a van that appeared to double as an ambulance. Birmingham was not there. She looked around, relieved when she saw Jackson climb in the back with her and pull the door to.

* * *

Clara sat on such a pristine white bed that she felt she was making the place look untidy. Whilst her favourite jumper, now torn from the crash, was cosy for a night in front of the TV, it looked out of place here surrounded by uniforms that had been ironed to within an inch of their lives. She wished she had had time to pack a bag, just to bring a change of clothes.

Her left arm was now in a blue fibreglass plaster. She had been told it was a clean break and should heal up well. The graze to her head had been cleaned, and a quick glance in the mirror had put an image to the pain. Her left eye was swollen shut, red and puffy with an outline of purple bruising that was starting to come out nicely. In short, she was a mess, and this was not exactly how she had pictured meeting her biological father for the first time. Clara gave the impression to the world that she had no interest in him, but it wasn't entirely true. As much as she fought against the idea, he was part of who she was.

The door to her room swung open and Jackson strode in. 'All fixed up?' he asked; rather unnecessarily Clara thought, since he was bound to have had a full report from the doctors. She raised her blue-encased arm.

'All done. How do you like the Air Force blue?'

She could have slapped herself in the head. What an idiotic thing to say! Still, she managed to raise a smile from him, even if was in sympathy at her poor joke. There was something about the way he smiled that made the world seem to stop. His eyes drew her in like a whirlpool, and she felt sure she would be happy to drown in them. As she watched him, he seemed to stiffen to attention.

'General Driscoll,' he said; by way of

greeting or introduction, she wasn't sure.

'Henry. Good to see you.'

The General, in full regalia complete with row upon row of medal ribbons, stepped into the room and offered Jackson his hand. Jackson relaxed slightly and shook it. Clara got her first look at her biological father in the flesh; but if she was honest, it felt no different from looking at a photograph of the man on the internet. He still seemed far away and unreal to her. After what felt like an age, the General turned and stepped towards the bed.

'Miss Radley,' he said, holding out a hand in such a formal manner that Clara could have laughed at the ridiculousness of the situation, had she not had every fantasy image of their reunion shattered in that moment. 'I'm General George Driscoll.'

She stared at the hand, not knowing what to do. She looked at Jackson for some sort of indication, but he was studiously avoiding her gaze, staring at the wall behind her head. She knew that she should do or say something, but the minutes ticked by and all she could do was stare at the proffered hand.

'Well, I imagine that you need to get some sleep,' the General said. His tone was even, but Clara wondered if she could detect the slightest hint of embarrassment. *Good*, she thought, *let him squirm a bit*.

'Actually, what I need to do is speak to my family,' she said, finding her voice at last. 'My mum and dad.' Clara watched for a response. She got none, and felt an unexpected stab of pain. Perhaps her worst fears had been right. He didn't want to be a part of her life — not back when she was born, and not now that she was adult. In fact, she felt sure she would never have met him if this situation hadn't arisen. She was merely a pawn in a game of chess he was playing with an unknown enemy.

'I'm afraid that's not possible,' he said. 'I've had assurance from the

British government that your parents and brothers are safe. That'll have to do for now.'

'I'm not one of your soldiers, General. I don't take orders from anyone.' The end of the sentence, *and especially not from you*, was unsaid; but Clara could see her inference was not lost on the uniformed man.

'You're right, I cannot give you an order, but I can strongly advise you against an action that could potentially harm your loved ones.'

Clara felt as if she had been slapped. This man, this man whose only contribution to her life had been DNA, was actually suggesting that she would put her family at risk, even after she had left everything and everyone behind to face who knew what danger, with the sole purpose of keeping them safe. Safe from a danger that was entirely of his own making! Her feelings for him before had been abstract and unconnected, but she now felt dislike grow inside her.

58

'Fine,' she said coldly. 'If I can't speak to them, perhaps you would do me the courtesy of telling me what's going on.'

'That's classified. You've been told everything that's necessary.'

Without waiting for Clara to speak further, the General turned to Jackson, who quickly stood to attention.

'I need to speak with you, in private. I'm wanted on the Hill, but I told them they could wait until I'd briefed you first.'

All Clara could do was stare. She wanted to say something, but she wasn't sure what, and she didn't know where to start. She looked over at Jackson, willing him to do something, anything, to make this embarrassing moment pass. And then he did.

'Of course, General. Shall we step outside?' Jackson looked over at Clara, but she couldn't read his expression. The General nodded his head in Clara's direction like a form of distracted greeting, as if she was one of his men returned from the battlefield instead of his long-lost daughter — whom he had never bothered to get to know up until this point; and now he had blown it. Well, Clara was done. The relationship had never even got started, and she was not about to make any more effort in that regard now.

Her anger, which had been kept in check by overwhelming fear, now flared. Thanks to the General, she was thousands of miles away from home. She had been dragged from her bed and her life in the middle of the night, been in a car crash, shot at, and bundled onto a plane to the States. But now she was done, done and going home. She was no longer convinced that she was in danger, or maybe she just didn't care. If the Close Protection Squad could keep her family safe, then they could keep her safe too. She wanted to go home and she wanted to see her family. To see her mum — and dad. Jason, the man who had raised her as his own and knew what being a father was really all about. The General could not keep her here against her will. She was a British citizen and she was going home, whether he liked it or not.

5

A nurse in scrubs walked in, interrupting Clara's thoughts. 'I have a change of clothes for you, ma'am,' she said, walking over and placing them on the chair. 'Just ring the bell if you need any help.' And with that, she was gone.

Clara slipped her legs over the edge of the bed and took a few deep breaths. She felt dog-tired. She reached over to the pile of clothes and realised that they were scrubs, like the nurses', only she suspected that these were what the military gave you as pyjamas. They were not going to be conducive to her escape, so she ignored them and walked over to the door. It was a sliding door of frosted glass, so when it was closed she couldn't see what lay outside. Cautiously, with her good hand, she eased it back and peeked out into the corridor. She had expected to see someone there guarding her, like on the TV, but there was no one; just an empty corridor and a repeat of doors like hers, some open and some closed.

She pulled the door open some more and slipped through, looking both left and right. Realising she was still alone, she slid the door closed. Hopefully this would give her time to find her way out before anyone realised she was missing. Padding down the corridor, she thought about what she was doing — or, perhaps more importantly, what she was going to do. She needed to find a phone so that she could call home, or call someone. If her mobile phone had been confiscated, it was likely her family's phones had too. She thought about calling Becky, her best friend, but how would she explain all this? Becky didn't even know that Jason wasn't her real dad. She shook her head, hating that term. Jason was the only 'real dad' she had ever known.

The sound of Army boots on the lino floor made her freeze. She looked for somewhere to hide, and, pulling open the door nearest to her, she slipped inside. She was in some kind of store cupboard that was full, floor to ceiling, with medical supplies. She slipped behind one of the stacks and crouched down. The noise of footsteps grew nearer and then stopped outside. She could hear voices, but they were muffled by the closed door, and she couldn't make out the words. She held her breath and willed herself to stay still. The footsteps moved away again and Clara let out a sigh of relief, even though she knew she was being ridiculous.

No one here wanted to hurt her. Just the opposite, in fact: they were trying to protect her. But she didn't want their protection. She wanted to go home. Just as she was thinking about whether she could slip back into her room unseen, the door opened and she ducked down, hoping it was a nurse needing supplies. It would be embarrassing to be caught sneaking around, and she could hardly claim she was looking for the bathroom, since her room had an en suite. The door clicked closed and she winced, hoping that whatever the person needed was on a rack near the door.

'Clara.' The voice made her jump and she tried to clamp a hand over her mouth to hold back a scream, forgetting that her left arm was in plaster and smacking herself in the nose with it. She let out a low moan, and the person in the door way was by her side in an instant.

'Are you OK?' Jackson asked in concern, running his eyes over her, efficiently checking her for injuries. All he could see was her uninjured hand held over her nose.

'No!' she said crossly. 'You made me jump!'

He lifted her chin and then reached for something behind him. Keeping hold of her, he tore the packet open with his teeth and pressed gauze to her nose, which was now bleeding. Clara moaned again under her breath.

'Did you fall?' Jackson asked, and she could see him fighting to suppress a smile.

'I didn't fall, I . . . ' She sighed again. There was no way she was going to keep her dignity intact. She took hold of the gauze, pressed it firmly to her nose and struggled to stand up. 'I hit myself in the face with my plaster.' She glared at him, daring him to laugh. Jackson, for his part, tried his best not to let his amusement show.

'OK,' he said, continuing to suppress a smile. Clara could see the battle for composure raging across his face. 'So what are you doing in the store closet?'

Clara fought the urge to come up with some plausible explanation, as she had never been very creative. Instead, she shrugged. 'Trying to escape.' She couldn't bring herself to look at him, so instead focused on her sock-clad feet.

'Escape? From what?' He seemed genuinely puzzled now. 'I'm just trying to keep you safe.'

'I know,' she said, shaking her head at herself. 'I just wish I was at home.' She had said it out loud and it surprised her, as did the emotion that welled up. She took a step back and turned away. The tears were flowing and she didn't want to embarrass herself further.

Jackson studied her for a moment. 'I'm sorry,' he said, and she could tell that he meant it. 'I know this has all been a nightmare for you. You must miss your family.'

The sob that she was trying to contain tore through her, and she could feel herself start to shake. His arms were around her again, and she buried her face into his chest. He didn't say anything, but rubbed a hand up and down her back, making her feel like a child in her father's arms. She wasn't sure how long she cried, but at last she felt able to pull herself together. She took a step back and the arms released her.

'Sorry,' she said. 'I've got blood on your shirt.' As she spoke, she noticed for the first time that he was out of combats and back in a suit, with a crisp white shirt.

'Don't worry. Occupational hazard,' he said, straight-faced but with a smile in his voice.

'Well, this is embarrassing,' she said out loud, as there was no point pretending it wasn't.

Now Jackson did smile. 'No one else needs to know,' he said kindly. But that was the worst of it — right now, he was the last person on earth she wanted to make a fool of herself in front of. 'As soon as it's safe I'll make sure you get to speak to your folks.'

Clara could feel the pressure in her eyes build up and she willed herself not to cry again. She couldn't believe how crazy her life had been over the last twenty-four hours. Her mind went to the source of it all. 'The General's quite a man,' she said, clearly not meaning it as a compliment. But if she was hoping to get a rise from Jackson, she was disappointed.

He could see that she was tired and

ragged, and he understood. 'Don't judge him on today. He truly is a great man, a man you can be proud of.' He tried to give a soft edge to his words, to reassure her.

'Shame the same can't be said for his parenting.' She wasn't sure why she'd said it. After all, it wasn't Jackson's fault that her father was so uninterested in her. Jackson clearly respected the General, and Clara didn't want to put him in this position. 'Sorry,' she mumbled.

Jackson lifted her chin so he could look her in the eyes. 'Just give him some time. He might surprise you.'

Clara closed her eyes to the wave of pain that came from twenty-five years of rejection from a man she had never met, now finished off with a bout of rejection in person. She'd told everyone who knew that she wasn't interested in her biological father, but it was amazing how much power a stranger had over you — how much they could still hurt you, even if you had decided to close off your heart.

'I am sorry, Clara, truly I am. We just need to get you safely through the next couple of days, and then, who knows?'

'Next few days?' she said.

'We think we're closing in on the perpetrators. If we can round them up, well . . . then we can look again at the level of security you might need going forward.' Jackson forced himself to look hopeful, even though he knew that he had just lied to her, and it wasn't the first time. He had no idea what the future held, but he knew that it was filled with trouble. The problem was so much bigger than just her, but he also knew that he couldn't tell her. What he had seen of her so far had assured him that she could handle it, but the General's orders were clear; and if there was one thing that Jackson accepted in life, it was that orders were orders.

'But if you catch whoever's making the threats, isn't that it? I can go home, go back to my life.' Even as she said it, a part of her — and she wasn't sure how big that part was — wanted to stay with

Jackson. She would never admit it, but she liked being around him. But his look was serious, and she knew more bad news was coming.

'The facts are out there, Clara. The world knows who you are and so the risk will always be present. We'll just be looking for a less invasive way of keeping you safe.'

He grimaced inwardly at yet more half-truths. He told himself it was in her best interests and necessary for the mission to be a success, but he still felt shame burn inside him. He watched as Clara's mind tried to process this latest bombshell.

She had been so naive, she knew that now. She had thought that when the threat was dealt with, it would be over. The realisation that it wouldn't was like a punch to the stomach. Her life was never going to be the same. She stepped away from Jackson, needing space and air. Then the lights in the cupboard fizzed and went out, and she felt Jackson step beside her. A moment passed, and dim yellow emergency lighting came on, directing them towards the door. A shrill sound filled the air and then the red fire alarm started to flash.

'Something's wrong,' Jackson said in a low voice, pulling Clara towards the door.

'A fire?' she asked.

He shook his head and pointed to the ceiling where Clara could make out a maze of thin pipes with holes. 'No sprinklers,' Jackson said. Carefully he crouched behind the door and pulled it open a crack before carefully closing it again. 'It's a trap,' he whispered.

'For the General?' she whispered back.

Jackson shook his head and he didn't need to say any more. She grew cold as she realised the trap was for her.

6

The storage room had no windows and so it was impossible to know what was going on outside. Jackson, however, pressed one finger to his left ear and seemingly spoke into the left sleeve of his suit. 'I have Blue Diamond. Please advise.'

Clara couldn't hear the reply, but the grim look on his face told her all she needed to know.

'We have to go,' he said in a low whisper. Clara could feel the tension coming off him in waves and knew that now was not the time for questions, so she just nodded. She watched as he searched the racks and found what he was looking for. He handed her a pair of pale green scrubs and a long white coat.

'Put these on,' he said before turning his back and searching the racks for something. Clara quickly slipped off her torn jumper and muddy jeans, wrinkling her nose at the state they were in and the smell that she hadn't noticed before. It was the smell of clothing that had been worn for too long, and that had not been designed for the activities it had been used for. The scrubs made her feel less dirty, but also more exposed, and somehow leaving her clothes behind made her feel as if she was turning her back on her old life. She felt as if she would never be going back. She fought the urge to take them with her and realised that Jackson was studying her.

'Here,' he said, holding out a brightly coloured surgical hat to cover her tangled hair. She blinked as she realised that he had changed too. His scrubs were pale blue, and despite everything going on, she could not help but take in the contours of his body. She turned her face away to hide the blush that was rising up her cheeks. Jackson, for his part, didn't seem to notice. He then took her by her good hand and pulled her towards the door, their only way out.

His look told her to be quiet and he cracked open the door. The shrill sound of the alarm was now joined by the sound of people hurrying to leave the building. It was a sort of orderly chaos, and Clara knew that it could help their escape.

'We're going to walk out following the rest. Keep your head down. Anyone looking for you will know what you look like, but try to act natural.'

Clara rolled her eyes at his mixed message. With a nod he stepped out into the corridor, and she joined him. He didn't hold her hand now but she could feel his closeness. The previously deserted corridor now held medical staff pushing beds and wheelchairs or helping individuals walk towards the glowing exit sign at the end of the corridor. In keeping with an Army hospital there was an air of calm, no shouting or screams of panic, and Clara could hear instructions ringing out down the corridor.

Jackson stepped behind a young man in a wheelchair and indicated to the nurse that he would take him. The nurse gave him a nod of thanks before turning back up the corridor and heading for another room to evacuate. Clara watched as Jackson surreptitiously scanned the crowds, looking for danger at every turn. When they reached the exit he grabbed a nearby orderly and whispered a command, before taking Clara by the hand and weaving through the crowd.

Once around the side of the building, Clara could see that they were making for the large car parking area to the left. There were no people here, as the assembly point was round the front, and she ran to keep pace with Jackson, feeling exposed in the open. A movement of air whipped her hair and she was pulled to the ground. She looked to see a dart lying just in front of her. She reached out for it, but Jackson knocked her hand away.

'Sedative. Don't touch, could be absorbed through skin. At least they want you alive,' he grunted, and then the sound of muffled gunshots filled the air. Clara hadn't been certain at first, since the wail of the alarm was being piped through the base's tannoy, but the hole in the side of a green Mercedes told her that someone was now shooting at her. Jackson dragged her around the side of the car as the whistling noise of bullets through a silencer slammed into the other side of the vehicle. The rear passenger window shattered overhead, spraying them both with glass. Jackson lay down and rolled under the SUV parked next to the Mercedes before pulling Clara after him. She watched as he crawled forward on his belly like an expert. She tried to copy him, but any pressure on her arm caused a flash of white-hot pain up to her shoulder, making her eyes water. She felt strong hands grab the top of her white coat and she was unceremoniously dragged from under the car by Jackson. He reached into his pocket with one hand and drew out an electronic gadget of some kind. He pressed it against the door lock and it sprung open.

'Keep your head down and sit in the footwell,' he whispered, helping her to climb into the seat of an old-model station wagon.

Clara scrambled across the driver's seat, listening to the sharp thud of more bullets against the cars around her. Thankfully, none seem to hit their car, and she guessed that whoever was after them was afraid of hitting her. It seemed Jackson was right — they didn't want to kill her. The thought that she was worth more to them alive than dead made her shiver. Crouching in the passenger footwell, she lay her head on the seat and watched as Jackson slid into the driver's side. Fear gripped her as she realised that he would have to sit upright to drive them out of here, putting him in real danger. He was the only person she could trust right now, and the thought of losing him sent cold stabs through her heart.

'Be careful!' she warned, and was rewarded with a grin. She shook her head. She couldn't believe it; Jackson seemed to be enjoying himself. She allowed herself to sit up slightly and peek over the dashboard. A firm hand pushed her back down.

'Stay put!' he ordered, all trace of humour gone now. He pushed the gear stick into reverse and swung the car in a wide circle out of its parking spot. The station wagon rattled as a few bullets found them, but thankfully all were wide of their human targets. The muffled whistling was now being answered by loud rattling bangs. Clara turned her head to Jackson.

'Ah, the cavalry,' was all he said, before making the wheels squeal as he drove out of the car park at full speed.

The car jerked as they hit speed bumps at full pelt. Clara felt as if she was sat in a washing machine on spin cycle. Jackson made the car swerve left and right. She could see blue flashing lights reflecting on the leather of the seat and just about make out the sirens over the engine's strained noises.

'Hold on,' Jackson said. Clara pressed her face into the seat and gripped the sides for all she was worth. There was a splintering crash, and Clara guessed they had just driven through the barrier at the entrance to the base.

'Why didn't you stop?' she gasped. 'Surely they could help us?'

'I've been told to go dark,' Jackson said. Glancing at her, he expanded, 'Go off the radar. There's a leak, Clara, and right now I don't know who I can trust, so it's just you and me.'

'Are we being followed?' she asked after she had time to digest this last comment.

'No; all caught up in the chaos back there I should think. But we need to ditch this car and find ourselves a new one that can't be traced.'

Clara carefully turned herself round and dragged herself up into the seat before pulling on her seat belt. 'Where are we going?' she asked.

'First we need distance, then a change of car and clothes. Then somewhere we can hide and won't stand out.'

Clara glanced out the window, taking in the highway before her. She had no idea where they were, but they certainly seemed to be putting some miles between themselves and the base they had fled from. 'And where would that be?'

'Where would an Englishwoman not stand out?'

Clara frowned and her face was a question.

'We're going to hide amongst the tourists. You can be the wide-eyed English backpacker, and I can be your American boyfriend showing you the sights.'

7

Jackson had pulled into the biggest car park that Clara had ever seen. It was like a huge ringed doughnut, and in the centre was a massive shopping mall. He had found an old jumper and sweatshirt in the back of their car. Clara pulled off the white doctor's coat and then slipped the sweatshirt over her head. It was far too big for her, but as Jackson had said, they now looked like medics who had just finished a long shift. The arms of the sweatshirt hung down and covered her hands as well as the bright blue plaster cast on her left arm.

Jackson caught hold of her good hand and started to walk towards one of the many entrances to the mall. 'First we need money,' he said.

'Well, don't look at me. I literally have the clothes I'm standing in, and none of them are even mine.' She grimaced slightly as she caught sight of herself in the window of a big department store. She looked like she had slept in her scrubs, which was maybe a good thing. At least she looked like she had genuinely been working all night. The long sleeve of the sweatshirt covered her broken arm, but nothing could hide the bruising around her eye and the swollen knot on her forehead. She looked like she had been in a car accident, which of course she had. She was aware that Jackson was looking at her too.

'We'd better get some cover-up as well. We need to go unnoticed. People are going to take one look at you and suspect that you're in trouble.'

He steered them towards an ATM and waited until there was no queue. Clara watched as Jackson looked casually around him. He didn't push a card into the slot, but entered a complicated series of numbers into the ATM keypad. Clara stared and wanted to ask what he was doing, but equally didn't want to draw attention. As casually as if he were out for an afternoon visit to the mall with his girlfriend, he pulled out the wad of cash that the machine offered and pushed it deep into the pocket of his scrubs. Then he turned and pulled Clara along and into the mall.

'I'm going to find you somewhere safe to hide and then go and get the supplies that we need,' he said, leaning in to her so that no one else could hear his words. He gave the impression that he was giving her an affectionate kiss on her cheek.

Clara felt her heart skip at his closeness and fought the urge to throw herself into his arms. It really had been a long forty-eight hours, and she needed to get some rest. If she didn't, she was likely to do something wild and impulsive, and she had a feeling that Jackson would be involved. She nodded, wondering where on earth he was planning to stash her. The truth was, although she didn't want him to leave her, she didn't think she wanted to wander around the shops waiting for masked gunmen to jump out at her.

Wide double doors to the left directed them to the toilets, and they followed the line of people down the corridor. Instead of peeling off left for the ladies' or right for the gents', they kept walking on through another set of doors. This door said 'Staff only'. Along the corridor were more doors, and Jackson proceeded to test the handle of each, finding them locked. Glancing about, he let go of Clara's hand and knelt down, pulling something that looked like a strip of metal from his right shoe. Within two heartbeats he had the door open, and pushed Clara inside.

Looking around, Clara could see a cleaning cart, and racks of cleaning supplies and toilet rolls. She was in a storage closet again. She turned to look at Jackson with a raised eyebrow. 'Really?' she asked. There was the ghost of a grin on his face, and she knew in an instant what he was thinking. She could feel two spots of heat on her cheeks.

'Stay here. The door will lock behind me. If anyone comes in, hide back there behind the laundry bins. I'll be thirty minutes max.'

At that moment her stomach gave a loud and unexpected rumble. Self-consciously she held her hand to her belly and willed it to be quiet.

'I'll bring some food, too. I don't know about you, but I never seem to have time for breakfast,' he said, heading for the door, his grin now evident. 'And, Clara — watch yourself with that plaster cast.'

Clara had to fight the urge to grab the nearest toilet roll and chuck it at his head. After he'd gone, she pulled a couple of clean towels off a nearby shelf and sat down. She could feel fear at the edges of her mind and she fought to push it back. It was a different kind of fear than when she was with Jackson, or even when strange men were firing guns at her: this was the fear of being alone. She wondered what she would do if something happened to Jackson, or if he simply never returned. How long would she hide out in this storage closet before she needed to make a break for it? Then what would she do? She had no money, no passport and no phone. Jackson had warned her that she could trust no one, and she had no idea whether this included the local police or not.

She could feel herself start to shake and knew that tears were not far behind. She needed to calm herself and think about something else, a trick she had used when she was a small child. But her childhood memories seemed out of reach, almost like they now belonged to someone else. All she could think about were the last two days, and that wasn't really helping on the fear front. Then her mind caught an image of her rescuer grinning at her in amusement. Jackson seemed to smile with his whole body. The image made the fear recede, and Clara brought her knees up and wrapped her arms around them. Her mind found another memory, one of strong arms holding her tightly and her face buried safely in his chest. She let her imagination run wild, and pictures of her drawing his face to hers and softly kissing his lips flooded her and pushed the fear aside.

She jumped as the door opened, and just in time remembered not to lift her injured arm to her face. The last thing she needed was another bloody nose — or, worse, a broken tooth. With light streaming in from behind, Clara couldn't see the man's face, but his shadowy outline was familiar to her, and she knew she was safe: it was Jackson. She let out her held-in breath and tried to push her fantasy away; to not think about his touch and how it made her feel. For not the first time in her life, she was glad that the people around her could not read minds. She watched as Jackson strode towards her, taking in his movements and watching for any sign that they were in imminent danger.

'Here,' he said, 'I brought you a change of clothes.' He handed her a bag and then moved to stand with his back to her. He had already changed into a pair of tight-fitting denim jeans and a black T-shirt. He looked younger somehow in casual clothes, and — although Clare tried to fight down the thought — like more appropriate boyfriend material as well.

She emptied the bag on the floor, and found not only clothes but also a change of underwear. She picked up the bra in surprise and looked at it, blinking when she realised that he had managed to pick the right size. She looked at his back suspiciously, wondering how he knew, and then forced the thought aside. Turning her back to him as well, she slipped out of the scrubs and underwear and chucked them into the nearest laundry bin. She pulled on the bra and pants, and then the blue jeans and flowery peasant shirt. She didn't need a mirror to know that she looked good, or that she would have picked out each item for herself had she been the one doing the shopping. When she was finished, she stood staring at Jackson's back, expecting him to turn round, but he didn't.

'I'm ready,' she said, although what for she wasn't sure. He turned slowly and his eyes seem to drink her in for a moment before he remembered himself.

'Here.' He handed her a light jacket. 'If you lay this over your arm, no one will notice the cast.'

She took the coat from him and allowed herself to be directed to a cardboard box, which he gestured for her to sit on. He pulled a tube of foundation from the bag and uncapped it. She couldn't help but giggle at the sight.

'What?' he demanded.

Clara put her uninjured hand to her face and tried to smother the smile. 'I never had you pegged as a makeup artist!' And then she allowed a further giggle to escape, so that she had to hold her sides to prevent herself from falling off the box.

'I am a man of many talents,' his said, wiggling his eyebrows, which made her giggle even more. 'Now, sit still and let me sort your face out.'

Clara obeyed, but couldn't shake the feeling of ridiculousness about the situation. Jackson was studying her face; she could feel his eyes take in every feature, and she was pretty sure it was not all about covering the bruises. She winced once at his touch, but knew deep down that it was for his benefit only. She couldn't feel pain at that moment, only the delicious sensation of his fingers touching her face. An image popped into her head of him holding her and his fingers tracing the outline of her body, and she forced her mind to stop.

He stepped back and said, 'Wouldn't stand close inspection, but it'll do for now.' He hauled her to her feet, then paused at the door to listen, and they slipped out.

Once they were out in the public area, Jackson slung an arm around Clara's shoulders and pulled her close to him. They strolled along, and it was only because Clara was paying him such close attention that she knew it was all an act. Occasionally he would pull her to one side to look at something in a store window, and she would play along with the charade. After five minutes she was almost convinced it was real herself.

Then, without any warning, Jackson spun her round and they headed into the perfume department of a department store. 'Fancy some lunch, sweetcheeks?' he said loudly and in a casual manner.

Clara was pretty sure that food was not on the menu. As they wove between customers and shop assistants, who threatened to spritz them with cologne at every turn, Clara hissed, 'What is it?'

'Couple at six o'clock.' Clara made to turn her head, but the sudden tightness of his grip made her stop.

'Keep moving,' he whispered. 'If we get separated, head for car park area G, black Ford Mondeo with Maryland plates.' She felt him push a single key into her hand. Where he had got it from, she had no idea.

From the muffled complaints behind her, Clara knew that the couple had picked up speed too. She risked a turn of her head and saw a man and a woman, dressed casually but walking briskly in their direction. Jackson had noted their quickening pace too, and pulled Clara forward. She knew that their cover had been blown, and whoever was following them was a genuine threat.

'We're going to head for the stairs. You keep going and I'll catch you up.' Clara wanted to argue but could feel the urgency in his voice. 'Find the car, get in and drive. Don't wait for me.'

'Where?' She had many questions, but somehow the instinct to get away was so strong that this one floated to the top.

'The car has satellite navigation. Follow it. I'll meet you at the destination in twelve hours. If I'm not there by then, drive to the next one.'

The fear was back, and Clara fought to keep herself from clinging to Jackson and begging him not to let her go alone; to come with her. But as he pushed the doors to the stairs open, she knew that this was impossible. The only way she was going to get away was if he stayed and dealt with the two people following them.

The doors swung back and forth behind them. Jackson kept pace with her down the first flight of stairs and then stopped. He pushed her roughly and then ducked out of sight, clearly hoping for an element of surprise.

8

Clara's feet moved so fast that she had to keep reaching out for the banister to steady herself, but somehow the adrenaline coursing through her veins kept her going. She heard movement above her — a muffled yelp and a crash, and then the sounds of fists meeting flesh. She willed herself to block out the sound, hoping against hope that Jackson had the upper hand.

She reached the bottom step and felt the jar run through her body as she made to take a step down that wasn't there. She felt a jab of pain from her ankle but ignored it, bursting through the doors and back out to the ground floor of the store. Everywhere she looked, there were household goods and appliances. She weaved in and out of the shoppers, resisting the urge to run in case she caught the eye of a store detective; the last thing she needed was to be stopped for suspected shoplifting.

The electronic back doors of the shop seemed to take an age to open, and Clara had to take a step back to avoid being clocked in the face. She felt the cold metal of the car key in her pocket and stepped out into the sunlight. It was brighter than she remembered, and she took a moment to blink and find her bearings. The instructions Jackson had given her seemed to have been seared in her brain. She looked up and saw a sign that read 'Area J'. With one hand shielding her eyes, she searched for an indication of which direction she should go in. To the left was a sign for 'Area K', so she moved quickly to her right. As she did so, a man who had been smoking a cigarette stepped in pace behind her. She tried to casually speed up, glancing at an imaginary watch and acting as if she was late for something. Chills ran through her as she realised that the man had increased his speed too.

She tried to scan the area for a black

Mondeo, but it seemed like the whole world had come to shop in their black cars today. In frustration she lifted the key to her face, wondering if perhaps it had a licence plate tag attached. It didn't, but she noticed for the first time that it had a plastic fob and it was electronic. As she moved through the car park, she pressed the fob button and waited for the tell-tale beep. Nothing happened, so she moved on to the next row of cars — again nothing. She daren't risk a look behind her, but she knew the man was still there. She wondered if she had it in her to fight him, or if anyone would step in to help her if she did.

By the second-to-last row of cars, she was getting desperate. Her fingers seemed numb and it was difficult to press the button. When a black car on the end of the row beeped, she had to fight back the tears of relief that threatened to overwhelm her. She dived off to one side and ran for the door. Yanking it open, she realised her mistake. She was in America and it was a right-hand drive, but she had opened the passenger door. She slipped the key between two fingers, like she had been taught in a self-defence class at university, and braced her feet. Swinging round, she prepared to face her attacker — but he was gone. She scanned the car park and then spotted him, embracing a woman before he stooped to lift a small child into his arms.

Clara thought her knees would give way, and she steadied herself against the door before forcing herself to close it and walk round to the other side. This man was clearly not following her, but it didn't mean that no one else was. She eased into the seat and adjusted it so that she could comfortably reach the pedals. When she reached out for the gearstick, she realised that the car was automatic, which would certainly make it easier to drive with one arm in plaster. Staring at the levers around the steering wheel, she quickly found the one she needed and pushed the key into the lock. The engine came to life, the central electronic panel flashed on, and a tinny voice told her to 'turn left and exit the car park'.

Clara allowed herself one glance in the rear-view mirror to see if there was any sign of Jackson, then pulled out of the parking space and into the steady flow of traffic towards the exit.

9

Only when she had been driving for over an hour without incident did Clara start to relax a little. As with most people driving in a foreign country, she was alert for the blue flashing lights and sirens that would tell her that she had accidentally violated some traffic law that she was unaware of. For Clara, this fear was more acute, as she was unsure whether the officer pulling her over would be friend or foe.

At first she was concentrating so hard on driving on the 'wrong' side of the road that she was oblivious to where she was headed. She had turned off the freeway about ten minutes previously and found herself on smaller and quieter roads. With few signs to give her any clues, and no idea whatsoever of the local geography, all she could guess was that she was heading somewhere out of the way and quiet.

She was desperate to use the toilet, but too afraid to pull off the road at a rest stop, and uncertain what might happen if she just stopped on the roadside. The world around her was familiar, yet alien, like a version of the English countryside but on a totally different scale. The wide-open spaces had slowly changed to woodland, and the view from the road became less expansive, with trees all around. The air seemed heavy and closer somehow, and a glance at the darkening sky told Clara that a storm was on its way. She only hoped she would reach her destination before it started.

The road ahead had a soporific effect, and Clara could feel her head start to nod in rhythm with the passing trees. The car jerked as she veered too close to the painted raised line that divided the road from the forest, and she forced her eyes wide open. The last thing she need right now was to fall asleep. She leaned over and pressed the button for the radio, but got nothing but static. Not wanting to risk taking her eyes off of the road to try and tune it in, she settled for rolling down her window, letting the freshening breeze jolt her back to wakefulness.

At that moment the satnav, which had been quiet for so long, intoned that she should take the next left. Slowing down, she could see what could only be described as a track winding off in amongst the trees. She flicked her eyes back to the satnav to check this was the correct turning, and then shrugged. Clearly Jackson's plan involved hiding out in the middle of nowhere — quite literally.

Darkness came down as if the man upstairs had flipped a switch. After several attempts, and having to listen to the windscreen wipers screech across the bone-dry windscreen, Clara managed to switch the lights on. The satnav was now telling her that she was just four miles from her destination, and she could have kissed it. To say she was tired was like saying the Sahara was a little bit dry. It was taking all of her willpower to stay awake, and she was starting to shake with the effort. The thing that kept her going was the thought that Jackson would be there at her destination, and he would make everything OK.

The track stopped abruptly, and Clara had to stamp on the brakes to prevent herself from driving into the hut ahead. She guessed it was some kind of camping/hunting lodge, but the Hilton it was not. The noise of the engine seemed loud in the forest, and for a moment she was worried that someone would hear her, which was closely followed by the fear that no one ever would. She was at least two hours from the nearest main road.

She flipped the lights off and allowed her eyes time to adjust to the darkness. The hut stood in a small clearing of tall pine trees, and this allowed a small circle of moonlight to reach the ground. Once she was certain that she would be able to see, she carefully opened the door and stepped outside the relative safety of the car.

She held her breath, but no monsters jumped out, and no wild animals appeared to ravage her, so she crept towards the front door. It was heavy and wooden and held tightly closed by a padlock. *Great!* she thought. It may not have been the Hilton, but the idea of sleeping in the car was not appealing, even dog-tired as she was. She racked her brains to see if she could recall Jackson mentioning anything about a key to this place, and then did a mental head-slap. They hadn't exactly had time to discuss the intricate details of their getaway plan.

She looked around the front door to see if there was a key hiding anywhere, under a stone or above the ledge, but there was nothing. Wearily, she turned back to the car. She was probably better off in there than out in the open, but the weather was close and heavy, and the idea of sleeping in a tin can — even with the windows open — was not a comforting thought. With a sigh, she decided to walk around the hut to see if she could see a more obvious place where a key might be hidden, or if there was a window that she could force open.

Round the back of the building, which was so close to the woods that it almost seemed a part of it, she spotted a rusted tin watering can. In desperation she picked it up, wondering if the key was hidden beneath it, but there was nothing but dirt imprinted with the pattern of the can. In frustration she dropped it, and heard a metal clinking noise. She picked up the can again and tipped it over; the metal clinking noise was back. When she tried to reach inside, she discovered her hand was too big to fit. Next she tried shaking the can, but nothing came out; whatever it was seemed to roll around on the inside like the last penny in a piggy bank. She shook it harder and harder, feeling herself getting pink and hot, hoping fervently that it was a key and not a stone or piece of broken metal. She was finally rewarded by a soft thump in the dirt, and there lay the key — or at least a key.

Clara scooped it off of the ground and walked back round to the front of the cabin. The sun was beginning to set, and Clara remembered how quickly it could become dark in this part of the world. She put the key in the padlock, and with some jiggling around she managed to pry the lock open. She pulled back the catch and pushed at the door.

The first thing that hit her was the smell. Like a combination of rubbish that had been left in a black bin liner in the sun for a couple of days, and the musty smell of a place that hasn't had its windows open for several months. She walked inside and took in the rustic look. It was all pretty basic, a mismatch of an old sofa and chairs and a scored wooden table that had seen better days with a bench on either side. There was a kitchen area towards the back of the room, with a cooker connected to a dusty bottle of gas and a worktop that had at least an inch of undisturbed dust covering it. There were a couple of cupboards, which Clara opened cautiously, suspecting that all manner of animals or insects might come flying out — but nothing. Just a collection of canned food, and a tin which Clara fervently hoped contained tea bags. Opening the tin, she found there was no tea but instead a strong smell of coffee; and she figured that coffee was better than nothing. Hunting around, she found some bottles of water and a kettle that would whistle when it was boiled.

She set the kettle on the hob and then returned to the car to see if there were any more supplies. Opening the boot, she found it was empty save for a jack and spare tyre. She picked up the jack, thinking it might be a useful weapon, and then dropped it again, thinking how foolish she was being.

Would she really have the guts to hit someone over the head with it, even to protect herself? She had always considered violence to be the resort of soldiers and men with no sense; but out in the middle of nowhere on her own, with no idea who was coming for her . . . well, that seemed to change things. She picked up the jack again, slammed the boot, and headed back in to the cabin.

She pulled the door to, but realised that there was no way to secure it, as the only lock appeared to be the padlock on the front of the door. Clara dragged one of the wooden benches towards the door and leaned it on its side, jamming the front door catch. It wouldn't stop someone determined from getting in, but it would at least give her some warning. The kettle whistled, and she made herself a black coffee before collapsing into one of the musty armchairs.

For the first time since she had left Jackson behind, she allowed herself to think of their last conversation. After twelve hours, if he didn't appear, she was to hit the road again. But was that twelve hours after they parted, or twelve hours once she arrived here? She tried to bring up his face, to remember what he'd looked like in that moment, to see if there were any clues, but it only made her feel more desperately alone. She wished he was here with her. Somehow this man she had known for barely forty-eight hours made her feel safe in a way that no one else could or ever had. It was more than that, she knew; it was not just about feeling safe, there was something about him that made her want to be by his side forever. She tried to convince herself it was all due to the stress that she felt that way, because his duty was to protect her and so she would naturally feel some connection to him, but deep down she knew. It was something she had never felt before, not like this. She was in love with Jackson Henry.

10

The loud crash made Clara fall off of the sofa. Despite the strong coffee, she had fallen asleep, and now she had tumbled onto the floor. She rubbed her left knee, wondering how many more bruises she was going to add to her growing collection before this was all over. Her dreams, which had had a nightmarish quality, started to fade, but left her with a dull fear and a sense of loss. She had been dreaming of her mum and the rest of the family; they had been reaching out for her, pleading her to help them, but however hard she tried she couldn't reach them.

There was the sound of wood grinding against other wood, and Clara's mind frantically processed the noise. Someone was trying to get in, and that meant trouble. Clara rolled onto her knees, ignoring the pain, and crawled towards the window. She didn't know why — it was pitch-dark outside, and there was no way that she was going to be able to see anything — but at least from this point when the door finally opened it would give her some cover, give her a few moments to work out what to do next. Her mind turned to the car jack, which she had brought inside for protection and left on the side by the cooker — too far away for her to reach, now that she needed it.

She held her breath and forced her nails into the palms of her hand to provide a distraction from the fear and to prevent herself from calling out. The door was shoved open, and the bench fell to the floor with a crash that made Clara jump once more.

'Miss Radley?' The voice was American, but softer than Jackson's, and she knew in an instant that it was not him. She was frozen to the spot; they had found her, whoever they were. She raised her plastered arm to her eyes when a bright flashlight found her face.

She felt rather than saw someone move to her side, and she tried to move away, but knew there was nowhere to hide.

'Miss Radley, I'm Special Agent Summers. Your father sent me.'

Clara blinked and tried to force her eyes to focus on the man before her. He was dressed in combats and a dark T-shirt, and was wearing a baseball cap.

'Where's Jackson?' was all she could think to say.

'He's been delayed, ma'am, so the General sent me to retrieve you.'

Clara knew a strong part of her wanted to believe him, wanted to believe that he was a 'good' guy and was here to help her . . . but she also remembered what Jackson had said, that she should trust no one but him. Agent Summers must have read the look on her face.

'Jackson Henry is a close friend of mine. We've known each other since grade school; joined up together too.' He smiled, and it seemed warm to Clara and his eyes seemed genuine, but still her mind would not let go of Jackson's words.

'He was delayed by the couple at the mall.' Worry passed across Clara's face.

'He's fine, they're both in custody, and Jack is hopeful that they will talk and then we can get to the bottom of this. If we leave now, we can meet him for breakfast.'

Clara allowed herself to be pulled gently to her feet; something about breakfast was sticking in her mind. Her stomach let out a loud grumble in response — probably just hunger, she hadn't eaten anything in what felt like an age. She was being directed to the door and her feet were following without her brain really registering what was going on. She forced herself to stop.

'Jackson told me to wait here for twelve hours; and then, if he wasn't here, to keep moving.'

Agent Summers smiled again. 'That sounds like Jackson, but we need to get moving. He was right about not staying in one place for too long.' He pulled her arm now, and in Clara's mind it was just a bit too firm. Something wasn't right, and that little niggle which she had tried to ignore was back and growing. She shrugged her arm free and turned to face him.

'I'm going to stay here, at least until the twelve hours are up.' She tried to put a firmness in her voice she didn't feel. She couldn't decide if she was being foolish and this man was going to turn out to be a friend of Jackson's, or if her instincts were right. He had said that Jackson was dealing with the couple at the mall, but if he was 'one of them' then he would know that the couple had been after them both.

'There's no point waiting, Miss Radley. I've already told you, Henry is interviewing the couple he apprehended at the mall — he won't be coming for you if you wait another eight hours or twenty.'

'Fine,' Clara said, folding her arms and taking a small step back. 'In which case, get him on the phone.' She wasn't sure what she would say to him if she got the chance. He would probably think she was even more foolish than he had previously considered, but at least she would know for sure.

Agent Summers smiled, but Clara could tell it was slipping a little. 'I already told you. He is interviewing suspects; he hasn't got the time to speak to hysterical damsels who are crushing on him.' The smile was mean now, and if Clara had her suspicions before, she knew it now: this man could not be trusted, and she sincerely doubted that he was a friend of Jacksons.

'You're not the first, you know. He's been on protection detail before. They all fall for him.' He grabbed her arm now and squeezed it tightly before dragging her towards the door.

'I don't suppose he has always resisted temptation. He has been in charge of some lookers, but trust me: spoilt, inexperienced English girls like you are so not his type.' He whispered the last sentence into her ear and she tried to pull away. She knew she couldn't trust this man, but his words were like a physical punch, and she felt some of the fight leave her. Of course Jackson would never be interested in her; she couldn't believe she had ever considered the possibility. But in the short time she had known him, he had taught her to fight, to believe that she was capable of looking out for herself. She looked around frantically for a weapon, but there was nothing. Then the memory of her bloodied nose swam into her vision. Pulling away again, she threw back her plastered arm and punched Agent Summers full in the face.

She was rewarded with cursing and a fair bit of blood, but most importantly he let go of her arm. The moment his grip was loosened, she pulled herself free and stumbled out of the cabin. It was dark and the moon was hidden by clouds but she forced her tired legs into a run. She couldn't see where she was going or what obstacles were in her way, but she knew what she needed most of all now was distance. She flew past branches that caught at her clothes and face, but ignored the stinging and pushed forward. As her eyes adjusted to the gloom, she could make out large objects like trees and take steps to avoid them; but low-lying branches and animal holes caught at her feet, and more than once she found herself face-down in the dirt.

She did her best to filter out the noise she was making charging through the woods, and to focus on any sounds that might indicate Agent Summers was hard on her heels, but with her breath ragged and her heart pounding she could hear nothing but herself. She forced herself to slow down and slid behind a tallish, broad-based tree. She focused on her breathing and demanded that her body take control again; she could feel the adrenaline making her shake, and squeezed her eyes tightly shut, trying to find a thought to calm her. A noise behind her made her freeze. Risking a glimpse in the direction, she thought she saw the momentary flicker of a torch. The sounds were moving closer, and she knew that if she ran now she would be caught. Her only choice was to stay still and quiet and hope she would remain hidden.

Clara tried to focus her eyes to scan around her, but the darkness was almost absolute as the tall trees blocked out any moonlight that could force its way between the clouds. Suddenly she was moving backwards, a hard hand clamped across her mouth and her arms pinned to her sides. She twisted and kicked out like a wild woman, but she could do nothing to make him loose his hold on her.

'Be quiet, sweetcheeks.'

Clara felt the fight drain from her as her brain managed to process the sound of the voice, and one word popped into her head — *Jackson*. She had myriad questions she wanted to ask him, but knew that it was not the time. She felt overwhelming relief at his presence, but the nightmare was not over. They needed to get away, on foot, and who knew how many of Agent Summers' people were out there looking for them? Henry held her close to his chest and waited a few heartbeats until Clara felt her anxiety levels drop, just an inch, and she started to relax, just a little.

He let go slowly and took her good hand in his. Clara could barely make out his face, but even in shadow she could see his focus. One tug on her hand and she was following him. She could see nothing, but he seemed to be able to move at such a pace she would have sworn he had night vision. After an age, with no idea of their direction or the time that they had been on the run, he pulled her down to her knees.

'Stay here,' he whispered in her ear, barely making a sound. She folded her arms around herself; the temperature had dropped, and now that she was still she could feel the coldness through her thin cotton top and jeans. Clara forced herself to count, and when she reached seventy-eight he appeared beside her again. As before, he grabbed her good hand and pulled her onwards. She couldn't be sure, but she thought the forest was thinning. The canopy above her head was now letting some of the waning moonlight through. Clara saw Jackson stretch out his hand and then heard a beeping sound which in the quiet seemed to echo all around her. She pulled herself closer to him, feeling sure that whoever followed them would hear the sound and zero in on their location.

'Get in,' he said, and then Clara could see the dark-blue truck in the shadows. Remembering for once that it was a left-hand drive, she walked around and climbed in. The truck leapt forward. Clara waited for Jackson to switch on the lights, but he didn't. He drove steadily, but at a far greater speed than Clara thought safe considering the dim light from the moon.

Clara clutched the sides of the seat,

ignoring the pain signals from her fractured hand. As the minutes ticked by and there were no ominous head-lights in the rear-view mirror, she tried to order her body to relax but it did not respond. The adrenaline that had coursed through her system started to fade, and she began to shake, feeling all the emotions and tiredness that it had masked for a short time. She felt a hand reach down for hers, without taking his eyes of the road, Jackson lifted it gently and Clara managed to let go of the seat.

'It's OK, Clara. You're going to be fine. We lost them.'

Clara tried to nod or say something, but couldn't.

'Did he hurt you?' Jackson's voice was tight now with anger.

'No,' Clara managed to say.

'I'm sorry that happened to you, Clara. I won't let it happen again.

'Not your fault.' Jackson's guilt was making her mind and body start to respond to her commands. She looked at his profile in the dim light and could see that his face was drawn and grim. With one hand on the wheel, he reached behind the driver's seat and pulled out a sweatshirt. He handed it to her.

'We're going to be on the road for a while, you should get some sleep.'

* * *

Jackson thought she might argue, but then the fatigue that she had clearly been fighting seemed to hit her; and within minutes she was asleep, her head leaning against the window. Her words rang in his ears: 'It's not your fault.' But he knew different: he should have been faster, smarter, better. If he had, she wouldn't have been so close to falling into the enemy's hands. He gripped the steering wheel, knowing that he would do anything he had to to keep her safe, and would allow nothing to get in the way of the singular goal — nothing. He forced his mind to think strategy. Summers' betrayal was a body-blow.

He had trusted Summers with his life many times, and vice versa. But recently there had been something slightly off about him, Jackson had put it down to Summers' recent break-up with his girlfriend but now he knew he had been wrong about that. Summers was one of them, he had sold his soul to the devil. For what? Jackson didn't know: money, perhaps, or maybe they had something on him. Some deep, dark terrible secret.

His attention turned to Summers' buddies but there were no red flags. Shaking his head he knew he would have to continue to trust no one until he had more intel. Looking across at Clara, he noticed the sweatshirt had fallen off of one shoulder, so he eased it up and tucked it in gently. He would do anything to keep her safe and if that meant being suspicious of everyone he had ever called 'friend', then so be it. He told himself that he was just doing his job, that she meant no more than that to him but he knew he was lying to himself. He shrugged as if trying to shake off the thought. He needed to focus on the mission — allowing his feelings to cloud his judgement would get them both killed. He gripped the steering wheel and made his mind focus on the information he needed to come up with a plan.

11

The motel was dusty from the nearby road and looked as if only desperate people would be prepared to stay there. The exterior was tatty and worn and made Clara wonder what the inside would look like. A large Alsatian-type dog was chained to the front porch of the tumble down wooden office. As they approached, he leapt forward, straining the chain and the rickety wooden upright that kept him where he was. He first growled, low and deep, and then his bark seemed to physically attack Clara and so she shrunk away, wanting to cover her ears.

'He won't hurt you,' Jackson said. 'But he'll let us know if anyone else turns up here.'

Clara followed Jackson up the steps and into the office. Any concerns that she had that they would be noticed and remembered left her when the office clerk did not even take his eyes off the TV — which, in the early hours of the morning, seemed to be playing an old 60s cop show — to take the cash and give them their room key. Jackson unlocked the door and gave it a push with his shoulder to force it open. Clearly maintenance was not high on the owner's list of priorities.

To Clara's relief, the room seemed clean, if rustic, and the smell that greeted her was one of bleach and polish rather than all the hideous things she had imagined. Jackson closed the door behind her and dumped the bag he was carrying on the small table under the window. There was, Clara noted, only one bed; but it appeared to be a king or super king, and she figured she was so tired she could probably sleep in the bathtub or on the floor if Jackson wanted the mattress.

'You hungry?' he asked, pulling a bag of crisps and a packet of cookies from the bag. 'It's not gourmet, but it's all I could get at the gas station.'

Clara smiled at him in appreciation. She didn't care about food, even though her rumbling stomach reminded her she had not eaten for some time. What she cared about was that she was no longer alone. She moved towards the table, feeling shy all of a sudden, and picked up a cookie.

'Are you OK?' Jackson asked. 'Did he hurt you?'

No. She shook her head, trying to figure out what question to ask first.

'Who was he?' She decided to go with the most obvious.

'Special Agent Brad Summers. I've known him since we were kids.' Jackson's face was set hard, and Clara could see flashes of anger fighting to be let out.

'Did the General send him?' She knew the answer already but somehow couldn't find the words to ask straight out if Jackson had been betrayed by a friend.

'No,' he said, turning his attention to unpacking the contents of the bag.

'I'm sorry,' Clara said, and she was; somehow she felt responsible, although she knew that it was not her doing.

'Don't be. We suspected that people close to your father were somehow involved; now we know.' He handed her a plastic bag containing a tourist T-shirt with a slogan about visiting the forest. Jackson thought about telling her how close he and Summers had been, how they had trusted each other with their lives, but thought better of it. It would not help her in her current predicament and would probably just make her feel more scared.

Clara moved beside him. However much he tried to shrug it off she knew he was in pain. She reached out a hand for his arm.

'Are you OK?'

'Shouldn't I be asking you that question? You're the one who I left to fend for herself.' He needed to keep the focus on her, could not acknowledge any feelings he had out loud about her or about the betrayal. If he did, he wasn't sure he would be able to hold it together. He set his face to neutral, as he had been taught, and flicked the switch in his head to close off all emotions.

She stepped in front of him, forcing him to look at her. 'You saved my life, *again*. I think that makes at least four times in the last forty-eight hours. So yes, I'm fine. Will you stop beating yourself up? It's not an attractive quality.'

She winced as the words left her mouth. What was she saying? She saw the anger fade a little, and some amusement soften Jackson's features — though whether he was laughing at her *faux pas* or at the idea of some attraction between them, she wasn't sure. She was glad, however, to see some of the old Jackson.

'Attractive quality?' he said, unable to keep a trace of amusement from his voice. He knew he shouldn't comment, but there was something about her that made her speak her thoughts out loud and he couldn't help himself.

'You know what I meant,' she said, in what she hoped was a suitably grumpy tone. He reached for her now and smoothed down her tousled hair before cupping her chin and lifting her face so that he could see it clearly. Clara could feel the breath still in her lungs and found herself studying his face, every curve, the small scar at his left temple. Without realising what she was doing, she lifted her plastered hand and traced her finger along the scar that cut through his right eyebrow. Their eyes locked together and it was as if neither of them could look away; they were lost in each other.

Clara tilted her head upwards and her lips found Jackson's as if they had to be together at that moment. She could feel him pull away slightly and so she slipped an arm around his back to secure him where he was. She pressed her lips to his and felt his resolve weaken as he responded in kind. The kiss was sweet and gentle as if they were both holding back — perhaps afraid of rejection, or maybe afraid that more would result in things going too far. As if in sync they both pulled away at the same time, breathing as if they had been running.

'We can't,' Jackson said; and although Clara's sensible side thought he was probably right, there was no way she was going to listen to him or herself. She pulled his face back to hers, and although she could feel some resistance, he found her lips again and this kiss was more intense, Clara could feel the heat rising inside her and knew that right now all she wanted was him.

She felt his hands on each of her arms, gentle but firm and he lifted her away from him so there was now space between them.

'We can't, Clara,' he said before moving his hand to gently smooth down her hair. He couldn't let her see how he felt. He couldn't let himself be distracted. He had to protect her, even from himself. If he let her know how he felt at her touch then they would be in even more trouble than they currently were.

'We can,' she said firmly, and made to step towards him again; but he held her back.

'It's my job, my duty, to protect you; and I can't do that if you distract me.'

Embarrassment flared inside her, and this quickly turned to anger. Agent Summers had known Jackson for many years, and maybe he had told her the truth about him, even if the rest of it had been lies. Maybe Jackson had been in this situation before, with other women — older, more experienced, more beautiful women. She turned her back on him then, as she felt her own foolishness was on display, and there was a small spark of anger. She was an idiot to read anything into his actions, to think that this was more than him simply doing his job.

Jackson stared at her back, stiff now as if he had physically hurt her. He pushed down the feelings of regret and the desire to feel her close to him again. His duty was to protect her, and he had told her the truth: he couldn't do that if they became more than what they were. What he didn't tell her was that he wanted to be with her too, to hold her in his arms and lose himself, to push away the events of the last forty-eight hours. To forget about betrayal and fear for a few hours. But this was not about him or what he wanted: he needed to protect her, and if that meant letting her think that he didn't care for her in that way, then that was what he needed to do.

'Eat,' he said, gesturing to the pile of snacks on the table. 'I'll make some coffee.' And he busied himself with that, allowing her time to compose herself — or maybe ensuring he couldn't see her pained expression, Jackson wasn't sure.

Clara tried to marshal her feelings. The weariness was back: she had held it at bay for so long but now it threatened to overwhelm her. She also knew that it was toying with her emotions, so she didn't really know how she felt about anything — Jackson, the General, what she had been through in the last few days . . . She forced herself to swallow and take a deep breath.

'I need a shower,' she said. Without looking at Jackson, she turned her back and headed for the bathroom.

'Wait.' His voice was steady as if nothing had happened between them; as if nothing had changed.

'What? I'm not even allowed to have a shower now? Or do you need to check with the General first?' She allowed the anger she felt towards her father fill her. Better that than the anguish, pain and embarrassment. She knew that it was the verbal equivalent of hitting Jackson with a stick but right now she didn't care.

She felt two hands on her shoulders and Jackson turned her round to face him, she looked away so that she couldn't see his face. She thought he might lift her chin as he had done before, but he didn't. Instead, he reached for her arm.

'You can't go in the shower with this.'

She looked at him now, doing her best to keep her face blank. 'Are you telling me that no one with a cast showers for six weeks?' She arched her eyebrow. Jackson smiled at her.

'No, people shower, but they usually cover their cast up before they do.'

Idiot! Clara told herself. Why did she always have to make herself look like such a fool, such a child?

Jackson pulled a roll of clingfilm from the brown paper bag. 'Got this at the gas station,' he said by way of explanation, and Clara watched as he gently covered her cast, taping the covering in place.

'Thanks,' she said, with what she hoped was an appropriate amount of grumpiness. She wasn't prepared to let him win her over like that, wipe away what had just happened between them. It had felt so real, so true, to Clara, and she could only hope that he felt it too, despite his denials. Jackson stepped away and she shuffled into the shower.

Twenty minutes later and she felt like a new woman, or at least a cleaner version of herself. She had taken her time. It had crossed her mind that she might be using up all the hot water, but the thought actually made her smile. She was sure that hardened military types were used to roughing it, and that a cold shower wouldn't bother Jackson, even if he would probably prefer a hot one.

She dressed herself in the T-shirt Jackson had brought for her. It was oversized and came down halfway to her knees. All she wanted to do was curl up in bed and sleep for at least twelve hours. Looking in the mirror, she took in the bruises to the right side of her face. The swelling around her eye seemed to have gone down, and she could open it a little; the colour was like a collection of autumn leaves, all yellows, greens and browns. She stared at herself: it was almost like looking at another person, or looking at herself in a dream. How had this happened to her? And, maybe more importantly, *why* had it happened?

She reached down for the plastic-wrapped comb and dragged it through her tangled hair. When she was as respectable as she was going to be, she unlocked the bathroom door and stepped out in to the bedroom. Jackson was sat at the small table, a large paper map covering its surface, eating some crisps. She closed the door behind her to announce her presence, although she was fairly sure it would be impossible to sneak up on Jackson.

'Feel better?' he asked.

'Yep,' Clara answered, and then made up her mind. She was certain that Jackson knew much more than he had told her, and that was about to change. She pulled out the chair opposite and sat down, then waited, expecting him to say something, but he continued to study the map. 'I need to know what's going on,' she said finally, fighting to keep her voice even.

'I'm looking at the best places for us to hide, which also happen to be the local tourist traps.' He glanced up for a second. 'How's your head feeling? There's Tylenol in the bag if you need it.'

Clara ignored his comment. 'I didn't mean what is happening right now. I mean that I want to know exactly what is going on. I think I have a right to know everything you do.' She crossed her arms across her chest, a little awkwardly due to the cast, and stared at him. Finally he sighed and looked up, before letting out a bark of a laugh. He coughed.

'Sorry, it's hard to take you seriously with that T-shirt on.'

She raised an eyebrow: she would not be jollied out of her mood or distracted by his handsome face and deep, warm laugh.

'You're right. That one's on me, I did buy it, after all.' He paused and studied her face. 'Four months ago, some information was discovered on the laptop of an individual high up in Army Counterintelligence.'

Clara nodded and helped herself to some sort of squashy cake that looked like a miniature swiss roll.

'The information was fragmented, and despite our best efforts, we were unable to draw any further information from the person involved.'

Clara raised an eyebrow, but decided that she didn't want to know the answer to the question that formed in her mind.

'From what we could establish, a group of persons unknown had established a network of individuals who had worked their way to be close to several key targets.'

Clara nodded. She knew this much.

'The targets weren't named, but from what we had obtained, we calculated that they were key people in the government, Homeland Security and the military.'

'So you thought that the General was

one of these targets?'

Jackson nodded and ate a handful of crisps. His face showed he was considering carefully what to say next. 'But we were wrong.'

'About the targets?'

Jackson nodded again and looked her straight in the eye.

'So instead of going after key personnel, whose security presumably had been tightened, they went after people *close* to the key personnel?' Clara gave an involuntary shiver as Jackson answered her question with a look of confirmation.

'Immediate family are given protection, but others aren't. The group have worked carefully to establish which relationships are most important, and targeted those with little or no security.'

'So, what then? Were they planning to ask for some kind of ransom or political favour?'

Jackson held Clara's gaze for a moment. The General's orders had been specific: Clara didn't need to know about the boy, it would only increase her anxiety. But then, Jackson knew the General didn't know or understand Clara. How could he? She was more like him than she would admit, and Jackson knew that she could handle the information he was about to give her.

'It's already happened, Clara. Ten hours before I came to extract you, the great-nephew of Senator Robinson was taken.'

'Great-nephew?' she asked in little more than a whisper.

'He's ten years old. Since there had never been any threat to wider family members, his family had no security. He was grabbed from his front yard. The ransom note followed thirty minutes later. Twenty-five million dollars, and the Senator has to vote against a key policy at the next weapons hearing in four days' time.'

Clara covered her face with her hands, managing this time to not injure herself with her cast. This was all so unreal, like watching a blockbuster movie at the cinema.

'As soon as the boy was taken, we knew we had made an error. The group were going after soft targets with minimal or no security.'

'So you came for me.'

'The General had me on a plane to England within the hour. The media have been in a frenzy — somehow, the identities of the key personnel have been leaked.'

'By who?'

'We don't know, but I suspect someone connected to the group. It's one of the oldest tactics in the terrorist playbook, spreading fear and panic to the nation without having to actually take any action.'

Clara frowned in confusion.

'Anyone, anyone at all connected to the individuals identified in the media, could be a target. *Anyone* connected in *any way*. The FBI, Army Counterintelligence, and even the CIA are doing their best, but there's no way to predict who might be targeted next, and we have no idea how to provide that level of protection. So the fear and panic spreads to everyone, and all the terrorist group had to do is kidnap one boy.'

'But you'll get him back?'

Jackson's face was set in a grim line.

'The Senator will pay the money?'

'We don't negotiate with terrorists, Clara. We can't. If we did, no one would ever be safe. You would never be safe. It would open the doors to any group with a gripe against the US. It's like saying, *Take who you like because you can rely on us to pay up and do what you tell us to.*'

Clara watched as he ran his hand across his chin, no longer clean-shaven but with a deep shadow. 'But the little boy?'

'We're working to get him back.'

Clara could feel fear clutch at her insides. She didn't know this boy, but she could only begin to imagine the anguish of his parents. 'What are the chances?' she whispered. He looked up and Clara held his gaze, willing him to tell her the truth.

'It's difficult to say.'

Clara pulled a face, guessing he was trying to keep her in the dark.

He shook his head as if to tell her that he was telling her the truth. 'Statistics for political kidnappings in the US just aren't available. It doesn't really happen on home soil.'

They sat in silence for several moments, each seemingly lost in their own thoughts. Then Jackson said, 'But from what I've seen so far of their operation, I believe that they'd be prepared to use lethal force to get what they want.'

Clara had to blink back tears. The idea of a small boy, terrified and alone, in the hands of men who meant him harm, who saw him as a pawn in their game, was almost more than she could bear.

'You look exhausted. Why don't you get some sleep?'

Clara nodded, feeling almost numb, like her brain had decided it couldn't take any more of this emotional roller-coaster she was on. She stood, and stumbled.

Jackson was by her side in an instant, guiding her to the bed. He pulled back the covers with one hand, keeping the other protectively on her back. Clara barely registered what was happening as the waves of fatigue swept over her. She was asleep before Jackson pulled the covers back.

12

Clara was running; it was dark as pitch. As she ran, she could feel the crunch of forest under her bare feet. She couldn't tell who was chasing her, or how many of them there were; all she knew was that she had to keep moving. Somewhere in the distance she could hear screams and she instinctively knew that they were from her mum and little sister, Tilly. She had to help them, but she had to get away from whoever was pursuing her too. The moon was hidden by dark storm clouds, and in the distance the rumble of thunder sounded like weapons being let off. She could feel the air pressure changes on her skin. She dug in, ignoring the pain in her chest and legs, her body telling her to stop but her brain refusing to listen.

She was alone, there was no one here to help her, and she didn't know where she was running to. She didn't know who she could trust; the fear was so familiar now it was almost a comfort. She heard a noise to her right, and automatically veered left without losing any momentum. In an instant she realised her mistake as something, a shadow that was somehow solid, loomed in front of her. She allowed herself a scream as hands roughly grabbed her. They were shaking her hard and she fought against them, lashing out and connecting with something real. Then there was light, bright and intense like she was under a spotlight, and a voice.

'Clara, wake up.' The voice was somehow both firm and gentle. Clara forced her eyes open and then she realised. She was in a bed, tangled in covers. Beside her on the bed was the figure from her dream, but this time she knew who it was. Jackson Henry sat beside her, holding her and whispering reassurances.

'Sorry,' she mumbled, 'bad dream.' Her sense of disorientation faded, to be replaced by embarrassment.

'I'm not surprised,' Jackson said calmly. 'You've been through one hell of an ordeal. A few nightmares are to be expected.'

Clara processed the comforting words until the last sentence. 'Patronising' would be one word for it. She eased out of his grip and fought to keep her face neutral. Reacting to what Jackson had said would only confirm his opinion that she was like a child who needed to be looked after and babied. She withdrew her hand from his and pushed back the covers.

'I've had worse,' she said. 'Some of the things I saw in Somalia and Nigeria would be enough to give even *you* nightmares.' She realised that she sounded petulant and that she was managing, despite her best intentions, to sound exactly like a child. Jackson nodded, showing no sign of amusement.

'I can imagine,' he said, his face displaying no trace of humour or teasing. 'You're not the only one who has nightmares, Clara. Most military personnel will tell you that they're haunted by some experience or other. We're only human, after all.'

Clara couldn't help but feel slightly mollified, though a part of her wondered if he was just saying what he thought she wanted to hear. This was annoying in itself, as he seemed to have her completely figured out, and she couldn't help but wonder once again if what Agent Summers has said was true, and that Jackson really was 'good with the ladies'.

'What time is it?' Clara asked.

'Oh-five-thirty.'

Clara tried to work out what the time would be in England. 'Can I use the phone?' she asked, though she knew the answer. Jackson shook his head but his face showed sympathy.

'It's too much of a risk, Clara. I'm sorry. They were safe and well before, and there is no reason to think anything has changed.'

Clara nodded. She hadn't really expected him to say any different; she just wanted to hear her mum's voice.

She watched as Jackson cleared the remainders of their supper from the table, dividing it into what they could take with them and what needed to be thrown in the trash.

'We need to be heading out shortly.'

'Where are we going?'

'I have a friend who I think can help us,' Jackson said, and she could feel him studying her.

'Can we trust him?' she asked.

Jackson paused and they stared at each other for a heartbeat. 'I don't know,' he said grimly, and Clara thought she could detect a trace of pain in his voice. 'But I don't think we have much choice. We can't stay on the run forever. The longer we are out here, the more likely we are to get picked up by the wrong people.'

'Then I guess it's a risk we need to take,' Clara said, although — and she didn't like to admit this to herself — the idea of being on the run with Jackson forever was alarmingly appealing.

By the time they had packed up their

150

limited possessions and dropped the keys through the office letterbox, Clara had come to a decision. If they were going to do this, they were going to do it together, and she was going to be an equal partner. She was going to start taking an active role in her own safety rather than letting Jackson do all the heavy lifting. She purposely walked around to the driver's side of the car.

'Wrong side, sweetcheeks,' Jackson said. 'You're not in England anymore.'

Clara stayed where she was. 'I can drive,' she said. 'The car's automatic, and I have a full driver's licence and everything.' She hoped that Jackson would get her sarcasm.

He folded his arms on the roof of the car and leaned in. 'You might have a licence, but I'm guessing you don't have it on you.' He raised an eyebrow. 'Unless you have it hidden in your cast.'

'So?' Clara asked.

'It's the law here. You have to have your licence with you if you're driving.'

Clara frowned.

'I'm guessing that's not true back home.'

She glared, then stomped around the back of the car and yanked open the passenger side door. She could have sworn that she could see Jackson's shoulders shaking gently, as if he were laughing at her.

'It's not that I'm saying you aren't perfectly capable of driving,' he said, turning the key in the ignition. 'It's purely about if we get stopped. I have a licence, you don't. If we get stopped, I can show them my licence, and we can be on our way without any trouble.'

She shook herself, trying to throw off her sulk. She knew he was right, but it was still intensely annoying. Driving was supposed to be her first step in asserting her independence.

They drove in silence for some time, and Clara figured that Jackson would probably be able to keep this up until they got to wherever they were going.

'So, where does this friend of yours live?'

'South Carolina.'

'And where are we exactly?' Clara didn't want to admit that her understanding of the geography of the US was sketchy at best.

'Virginia. We're heading for the Blue Ridge Parkway, where all the tourists go.' He took his eyes off the road long enough to flash her a grin.

'Is the tourist thing really a good idea?'

'An American travelling with an English girl — it's going to be the best place to hide. No one will give us a second glance, let alone remember us. And it's not the obvious choice for getting away.'

'Why?' Clara asked, deciding to ignore the 'girl' comment.

'The parkway has speed limits. Most people in our situation would head out for the freeway and eat up the miles.'

Clara nodded. 'So if anyone is looking for us, it won't be here, it will be further afield.'

'Exactly — or at least that's the plan.'

'But if we're being followed by people who potentially know you, may be even friends, won't they guess this is where we are heading?'

'I doubt it. It goes against all protocol; and besides, anyone that knows me knows that I'm not a big fan of the great outdoors.'

'I thought all you Army types loved all that hunting, hiking, getting-back-to-nature stuff.'

'Not me. I grew up in New York City. I'm a city boy at heart.'

Clara took some time to process this information. She'd been sure he would be the classic Army guy who loved being outside, living off the land — all of that outdoorsy stuff.

'So you're not from a service family?'

'No. My dad was a teacher and my mom was a waitress in a diner.'

'So how come you joined the Army?'

Jackson shrugged. 'Wanted to serve; to do something that matters.'

Clara nodded. This was something she could understand. When she was eighteen, she had volunteered at an orphanage in Romania, and after just a week had known what she wanted to do with her life. She had discovered the need to do something of value and make a difference.

'Penny for 'em?'

'I was just thinking about the first time I volunteered. I was eighteen, just finished school with no clue what to do with my life. I went on a week-long trip to Romania, working with children in an orphanage.' Clara could see the look of admiration on his face and she hoped sincerely that the warm glow she felt inside didn't reach her cheeks. 'I thought it would be fun — you know, playing with the kids and generally having a good time.' She stopped and Jackson seemed happy to let her remember. 'Couldn't have been more wrong, of course. The conditions were appalling: they had no facilities, not enough food or medicine. We did what we could, but I knew that I wanted to do more.'

Jackson nodded his understanding.

'So I went to university and studied international development and disaster management, spent two years in Somalia and then Nigeria, and now I'm working on my PhD in the same.'

Jackson's eyes were fixed on the road, but he didn't display any hint of surprise, although she could tell he was listening.

'You knew?' she said. 'How?'

Jackson laughed. 'The General told me. He's a proud father, you know.'

Clara took a moment to take this in. The General knew about what she had studied and what she had done with her life. Her mum had never mentioned that he had been in touch. Somehow, she was a little surprised that he was proud of her dedicating her life to charity work; that didn't really fit with the limited picture she had of him in her head.

'How long have you known? About me, I mean?'

'Three days.' He turned to look at

her to check that she was handling this new information OK.

'I don't think the General had told many people that he had a daughter.' She felt the all-too-familiar sting of rejection.

'Clara, I honestly think he was trying to protect you. Protect you from something like this.'

She swallowed and fought to keep her emotions in check. 'So you think that for the last twenty-six years he has been worrying about this exact scenario? You think that's what can explain away all the years of my life with no contact, nothing?'

Jackson didn't comment on her outburst, but lifted his hand off of the steering wheel and reached out for hers. She didn't shrug him off this time, feeling in desperate need for some comfort.

'I can't answer for your father, Clara. I wish I had answers for you, but I hope that once this is over you will at least give him the chance to explain.'

Clara couldn't find any words to say. Her mind buzzed with new information and old hurts, but one thing she did know was that if Jackson asked her to give the General a chance, then she would. In an odd way, she felt she owed him that much after all he had done for her. Even if Jackson seemed to see the General as some sort of hero rather than a deadbeat dad in a uniform, she would give him one more chance — assuming they got through whatever it was that lay ahead of them.

13

They drove for another hour in silence. Jackson had attempted to find a radio station to distract them both, but all they could get was static. Jackson's sigh told Clara that he was thinking they wouldn't be having this problem if they were in the city right now. Clara wasn't bothered by the silence; she let her mind drift. She had tried to sort the events of the last few days, and her feelings for the General and Jackson, but they all threatened to overwhelm her. Instead, she focused on the scenery around her. America seemed so vast in comparison with home. Everything seemed to be on a much grander scale. The road wound through wooded areas, and Clara could see repeated rocky outcrops and green, tree-covered mountains as far as her eyes could see. Overhead, birds wheeled and called, and although they were travelling on a well-kept road, Clara could not shake the feeling that the wilderness was just outside the car. It was strange, but somehow that made her feel safer and more hidden. Then a thought struck her. It had been nagging at the reaches of her mind, but with all the other things going on, she had not been able to pin it down.

'If the General has never told anyone about me, that he even has a daughter, then why would he be worried about my safety now?' Clara stared at Jackson and felt sure she saw him flinch under her gaze.

'Let's just say you made the news.'

She frowned. 'It made the papers?' She couldn't believe that the public would be that interested. It wasn't like the General was a famous movie star or something.

'Not just the papers, Clara. It's all over the internet, and every domestic news station started to run the story.'

She tried to take this all in; she

honestly couldn't believe that her life could get more surreal.

'The information they had been given was limited, and of course no-one was prepared to reveal their sources. The majority claimed they received an anonymous email with an untraceable IP address.'

Clara considered this new information. 'Do you think that was all the information they had?' She gave an involuntary shiver; the idea that the group behind this knew where she lived, knew anything about her, was terrifying.

'I'm beginning to doubt it,' Jackson said with a shake of his head. He glanced at her. 'I'm starting to think they couldn't find you, so they leaked the information they did have to force the General's hand.'

Clara felt as if she had been thrown into an icy pool. The cold was sudden and painful and almost took her breath away. 'They wanted him to bring me here,' she said in a whisper.

'It would certainly explain why they were able to find us so quickly at the base. To plan an attack of that magnitude takes time and money.'

'And an inside man or woman?' Clara asked. Jackson simply nodded. 'Do you think Agent Summers is the only one?' He shook his head. 'So we really don't know who we can trust.' The magnitude of what she was hearing was starting to hit home. Even though Jackson had said little about him, his pain told her that Summers had been a close friend and ally. His betrayal was bad, but the knowledge that their enemy could be anyone was worse.

'Other than the General, I would say any individual — known or otherwise — needs to be approached with extreme caution,' Jackson said, interrupting her thoughts.

Clara could have laughed: not that it was funny, just ironic that the only two people in the world she could trust right now were a man she had known for a little over three days, and a man who had never bothered to meet her, despite the fact that she was his only child.

'It may be that they consider they have achieved their goal and won't take any further action against you.'

Clara looked at him, her face a question mark, and she could see her own doubt reflected in his serious expression.

'The General is certainly distracted. A key member of his team has just revealed himself to be a traitor. He is a professional, of course, but his focus is divided and it may be that was all they wanted.'

'You might want to try a bit harder to convince your face,' Clara said, and she couldn't help but smile a little. She watched as he raised an eyebrow and then smiled too. Clara felt her heart contract and she knew his smile was genuine — slightly lopsided, but his whole face seemed to change with it.

'OK,' she said in a determined manner. 'So it's probably not sensible to assume that 'they' — ' She made two inverted commas with her fingers. ' — are no longer after us.' Jackson nodded in agreement. 'So, how long is it going to take us to get to South Carolina?'

'Who said we were going there?'

'Er, you did. To meet with your friend/contact/whatever. Are you so tired from driving that your memory has been affected?'

'No, sweetcheeks, the memory's fine. We're not going to her house to meet her. We're going to meet her somewhere much safer that also has a great view.'

Clara's brain wasn't interested in the last part. It *was* in the first part. Jackson's friend was a woman! She had assumed it was a man, and he had let her. She turned her head and pretended to look out of the side window and take in the view. She could feel colour and heat rising on her face, and didn't want him to see it. If this woman was someone Jackson felt he could trust above all others, then they obviously had history — and if Agent Summers had been telling the truth, then *history* could only mean one thing.

14

The hours seemed to pass in a blur. The landscape shifted from sheer rocky outcrops to more dense forest, and then back again. They travelled at a steady pace, and although the roads were not quiet, they were untroubled by other drivers who seemed keen to drive slow enough to take in the surroundings. Every few miles, the road seemed to wind around the outside edge of another mountain, and the forest would melt back, revealing views that seemed to continue to the other side of the world. The scale was breathtaking, and Clara decided that being on the run in such beautiful surroundings was not as bad as it might have seemed. Many of their fellow travellers stopped frequently to take in the views or enjoy a meal at some of the small roadside diners, but Jackson kept driving.

When Clara's stomach had rumbled so loudly that it sounded like thunder was heading their way, Jackson finally stopped. The diner was small and rustic, but the car park suggested it was a favourite with locals and tourists alike.

'Are you sure it's safe to stop?' Clara asked, suddenly feeling less hungry.

'We have to eat, and your stomach is telling me I have been remiss in my welfare detail.' He took the keys from the ignition and turned to face her. 'It's fine, Clara. We're boyfriend and girlfriend on a trip, taking in the sights and in need of some refreshment. Just relax and act natural. Trust me, no one will remember us after we have gone.'

Jackson stepped out of the car and walked around to the passenger side. Clara sat motionless; all feelings of hunger had receded, to be replaced by the overwhelming need to stay in the car where it was safe. She looked up as Jackson opened the door and held out his hand. His face smiled, but Clara could see tell-tale signs of tension around his eyes.

'Come on, sweetcheeks,' he said as she took his hand. When she was standing, he draped an arm casually over her shoulder and leaned in to whisper in her ear, 'Relax, Clara. We're on vacation and in love, remember?'

Clara could feel the warmth of his body next to hers. Her knees felt suddenly weak, and she knew it had nothing to do with fear. Her brain was telling her he was acting, that this was part of his job of keeping her safe, but her body was having a completely different reaction. She allowed herself a small smile, and decided that she might as well enjoy this closeness; even if he was pretending, she knew that she wasn't. She slipped her arm around his waist and hooked her thumb through the belt at the back of his jeans. He raised an eyebrow, but said nothing, and they walked together to the diner.

The diner was nearly full, but there was a seat by the window which afforded views of the surrounding scenery: tall trees with glimpses of the panoramic views beyond. Clara was surprised when Jackson asked for the table towards the back of the diner, which had views of the parking lot and was close to the swing doors to the kitchen that opened and closed every few minutes. Jackson turned on his best smile and the waitress didn't question his choice, but led them to the back before handing them two menus and reeling off the specials for the day.

When she had gone, Clara studied the menu. She was officially starving, and now she thought about it, she hadn't had a proper cooked dinner for four days. The smells from the kitchen were enticing, and Clara knew she was going to have difficulty making her choice. In the end, she went for the obvious: cheeseburger and fries with a side of onion rings. She figured that her lack of food for the last few days meant she could splurge a little. When the pretty waitress returned, Jackson ordered the same.

'I thought you would be more of a

169

salad gal,' he said, leaning in close — whether to give the impression that they were having a romantic meal or because he genuinely wanted to be closer to her, she couldn't tell.

Clara arched an eyebrow. 'Are you suggesting I'm fat?' she asked in mock outrage; she knew that she wasn't. Clara tried to take a sensible approach to food rather than the continual dieting roundabout that some of her friends back home were on.

She was rewarded with a laugh. He shook his head. 'No; just not used to women ordering the same as me.'

'Well, I think that says more about the women you've had dinner with than me.'

'You're probably right,' he said — a little ruefully, Clara thought.

She shrugged. 'I like food, and I'm happy with the way I look. I guess spending time in other countries gives you a bit of a different perspective on life and food.'

Jackson took a sip from the glass of

iced water on the table in front of him, but Clara could tell that he was only half-listening. She followed his gaze and realised that he was studying the cars coming in and out of the parking lot. She reached across and squeezed his hand in what she hoped was a flirtatious manner, just in case anyone was watching, of course — and whispered, 'Everything all right?'

Jackson's smile was tight, and he turned his face so he was staring at her. He leaned in and kissed her cheek.

'Not sure.' His breath tickled her cheek. 'Smile as if I've said something funny.'

Clara forced herself to giggle, but to her own ears it sounded fake and a little high-pitched.

'Do you see the Ford pick-up in the lot? Dark blue with Rhode Island plates.' Clara shifted in her seat and allowed her eyes to flick to the parking lot.

'Uh-huh,' she said.

'Can you see who's getting out?'

Jackson murmured as he picked up her hand and kissed it playfully.

Clara leaned towards him and planted a kiss on his cheek. 'Two men, dressed casual but not your typical tourists.' Clara did her best to appear relaxed, but she knew she was probably making a spectacle of herself. This undercover secret stuff was clearly not her natural calling. The waitress arrived and placed two plates laden with food in front of each of them.

'Can I get you anything else?' she said in a drawl. Clara suppressed the urge to say *Yes, get out of the way!* And managed to smile and shake her head.

The door to the diner opened with a jingle of bells, and Clara felt herself stiffen in her seat. Putting aside all caution, she stared directly at the door and felt Jackson's shoulders start to shake beside her. Two men walked in, and each had hold of a small child's hand. They smiled at the waitress and then took the table at the front with the good view.

'OK, so maybe we're getting a little paranoid,' Clara said, feeling embarrassed but somehow all right with that as Jackson had been the first of them to be concerned.

'Well, the thing to remember is, just because you're paranoid doesn't mean people aren't after you, sweetcheeks.'

Clara rolled her eyes. Her appetite seemed to return in a rush and she dug into her food, wondering when she would get to eat another hot meal.

15

They spent another night in a motel, this one with dodgy plumbing, and were up and out at six. Clara was untroubled by nightmares, or at least by nightmares that she could remember. When she woke, she felt as tired as if she had been asleep for mere moments, and she wondered if she would ever adjust to life on the run as Jackson seemed to have done. She had not seen him sleep since she had met him, although she guessed by now he must have had the odd catnap but he seemed permanently refreshed — which, Clara had to admit, was beginning to get a bit irritating.

After a couple of hours on the same long winding roads through the peaks, they started to pass signs for Grandfather Mountain. The signs indicated views and a place to stop and enjoy the park as well as to purchase the mandatory souvenirs. There was a small queue of traffic to get into the parking lot, and Jackson followed the car in front patiently, seemingly unconcerned by the upcoming meeting. Clara, on the other hand, could barely keep still. She wasn't sure whether it was the thought of meeting this mystery woman from Jackson's past or the threat that maybe she would betray them which was causing her the most worry.

They queued again with the other tourists — who, judging from the range of accents, were from across the US and beyond — and bought tickets. Jackson kept close to Clara's side and his presence was a comfort, if a little distracting.

'Do you feel like a coffee, sweet-cheeks?' he asked.

Clara fought the urge to glare at him. 'Oh, I'd love one, sweetie-pie.' As she said it, she leaned in to him and rubbed a hand on his stomach. Again the rumble of laughter.

'Now who's overplaying the act?' he whispered into her hair before kissing her lightly on the ear.

'Just acting my part as your ditzy English girlfriend,' Clara said with a sickly smile on her face. 'Isn't that how all your girlfriends talk?' she asked innocently with her eyes wide open.

'Not since fifth grade, no,' he said. Clara watched as he scanned the crowd of people milling around, waiting for friends to use the facilities or studying the map of what to do on their visit.

'Do you see her?' Clara asked.

Jackson shook his head. 'She'll find us; that's protocol. Let's get a drink and then head up to the bridge. It should be quieter up there and I'm told there are some great views.' He grinned at her and then led her by the hand to the coffee shop.

Jackson had been right — the views were stunning. Rolling hills with tall green trees, mountain ranges, and Clara could pick out the tarmac winding parkway road leading off into the distance. She made herself focus on the views; but, as amazing as they were, they could not completely distract her from the many families that were also visiting the mountain, and she had to keep pushing down the images of her mum and dad and the kids. She shook her head. Jackson was right: they were safe, and that was all that mattered.

'Excuse me, but would you mind taking a photograph of me and my girlfriend? She'd like to send a picture of us to her folks back home.'

Clara turned her attention back to Jackson, who had spoken, and took in a tall woman with pale blonde hair that looked annoyingly natural. The woman was dressed in jeans and a parka jacket, and looked every inch the fellow tourist. As she turned, Clara got a glimpse of her in profile, and could see how beautiful she was — and how tall, only a few inches shorter than Jackson's six feet or so. She smiled back at Jackson.

'Of course. Huddle in now. We want

to get you both in, plus the amazing view.' She lifted the cheap disposable camera in front of her face and Jackson put his arm around Clara's shoulder like a brother would do to his kid sister. In that instant Clara felt her hackles rise. He was treating her differently; no longer were they playing the part of boyfriend and girlfriend, now they were like family, connected but distant somehow. Clara had the sinking feeling in the pit of her stomach that the reason for this sudden change was standing right in front of her taking her picture.

Clara didn't need to ask if this was their contact; she just knew. She waited for the flash to fire once, and then twice for good measure. Jackson detached himself and strode over to the woman.

'Have you travelled far?' the woman asked.

'Yes ma'am,' Jackson answered. 'Well, me, not so much — I'm from New York State — but my girlfriend here is from all the way over the ocean.'

Clara had had enough of watching,

and besides, she wanted to know what was going on, so she stepped forward, smiling and holding out a hand.

'I'm Clara,' she said, 'from London.'

'Nice to meet you, Clara. I'm Annabel. I live in South Carolina, but decided to take a trip up the Blue Ridge Parkway, much like yourselves. One of those things, you know. I live so close, but I've never gotten around to it till now.'

'We're heading south,' Jackson said. 'Any suggestions as to where we might want to visit or stay? I mean, we've got the book, but sometimes local knowledge can be better.' Jackson smiled warmly and Clara knew that anyone watching would see three tourists swapping stories.

'Well,' Annabel said, giving the world the impression that she was considering the matter carefully, 'I wouldn't miss Asheville if I were you. Great city, wonderful places to eat, and of course the Biltmore Estate is not to be missed.'

'Thank you, Annabel. Much appreciated. You have a good day, now,' Jackson replied. Annabel smiled and then swiftly disappeared back across the bridge and into the visitors' centre.

Clara grabbed Jackson's hand. 'That was it?' she asked incredulously.

'Got all the information we need,' he said quietly.

'Well, if you've seen enough, sweet-cheeks, I vote we hit the road.' This comment was louder, and Clara felt sure it was not for her benefit. She nodded, feeling quite mystified, knowing that she was only going to find out more once they were safely back in the car.

Clara kept quiet as Jackson negotiated his way out of the parking lot and back onto the parkway. She knew him well enough by now to tell that he was focused on keeping track of everyone around them — scanning for signs of danger, no doubt. When they had been on the road for half an hour, it became clear that he wasn't just going to volunteer the information, and she sighed inwardly.

'So what's the plan?' She tried to

keep her voice neutral as if she were just mildly curious rather than desperate to know what was going on.

'We're heading for Asheville. Supposed to be a great city, don't you know?'

Clara frowned; that wasn't exactly what she'd been expecting. She had figured that all this cloak-and-dagger stuff meant that there was a secret meaning in his conversation with the mystery woman, not that what she was saying was actually what she meant.

You're kidding!' she said incredulously. Jackson just raised a questioning eyebrow. 'Wow. If I knew all this spy-secret-agent stuff was this easy, I would've joined up myself.'

'Well, it's not like it is in the movies, you know.' Jackson gave a small chuckle.

'But anyone could have overheard you!'

'If anyone cared, then yeah, I guess. But I don't suppose that any of our fellow tourists were that bothered, unless they were looking for a bit of local knowledge too.'

Clara could feel herself struggle with this concept. She had trusted this man with her life, and up till now he had seemed so cautious, so on the ball; but now — well, now she had the feeling that she would be safer on her own.

'How do you know they were all tourists?' She tried to keep her voice even.

'Jess wouldn't have approached us unless she had checked everyone out.'

Clara took a moment to digest this information. 'So she's in the military too?' She could curse her own curiosity. She knew she sounded too interested, and knew she was giving Jackson a peek at her own feelings for him, but couldn't help herself.

He laughed, and Clara turned her face away to take in the view and hide the signs of her feelings which she knew were crossing her face. He was laughing at her, just like an older brother might do with his little sister.

'Jessica in the military? Not a chance! She doesn't really do rules.'

Clara was desperate to ask more, to ask how he knew her — and, more importantly, what his relationship with her was — but she settled on a question that she figured anyone in her situation might ask.

'Can you trust her?' Now she forced herself to turn and look at him; she wanted to see his face when he answered her. To see the truth there, even if she couldn't hear it in his words. He didn't say anything for a few beats.

'Truth?' he asked, and she nodded.

'If you would have asked me four days ago who I trusted most in this world, after the General, I would have said Summers . . . but now I just don't know.' The silence stretched between them as Clara watched the pain of betrayal flash once again across Jackson's face. She reached out for his left hand, which he had rested on his knee, and gave it a squeeze. More than anything, she wanted to say something to take some of the pain away, but knew there was nothing to be said. Just as her world had been ripped apart by recent events, she knew his had too. This was something they shared, even if she felt more for him than he did for her.

Jackson took his eyes off of the road for a few seconds and their eyes locked. Clara knew she was probably imagining it, but she felt like more was said in those few heartbeats than at any time before. She knew she might be reading something into that look that wasn't there, but she felt a tiny glimmer of hope. If they got through this in one piece, maybe there could be more to them than there could be right now.

Clara was suddenly forced back in her seat as Jackson pressed the accelerator to the floor and yanked his hand free from hers, needing two hands to control the now-speeding car. On instinct, Clara checked out the side mirror and saw a black SUV hard on their heels. Just one thought passed through her mind: they had found them.

16

'Is it them?' Clara asked in little more than a whisper, she felt as if all breath had left her body.

'Well, it sure isn't someone wanting to ask directions,' Jackson said in a fake drawl. Clara flinched at his words; it felt like he was blaming her, maybe for distracting him for those precious few seconds.

The car swerved around a much older station wagon loaded with camping equipment and Clara had to grab the door handle to stay upright. Glancing in the mirror she could see the black SUV repeat the manoeuvre, keeping pace with them with ease. She heard a distant horn sound as the station wagon driver expressed his opinion of people who drove like lunatics on a serpentine one-lane road through a national park.

Clara kept a grip on the door handle,

despite the fact that the road ahead was relatively straight. What she really wanted to do was to hold on to Jackson, but she knew that was foolish in more ways than one. Her job right now was to sit still and shut up, to be as least distracting as possible. The road started to bend to the right and the few cars in front were bunched close together, slowing down for a rest stop. Jackson floored the accelerator and steered the car onto the wrong side of the road, and Clara had a flash of being at home, driving on the left. A minivan suddenly appeared on the road in front of them. Clara caught a glimpse of the driver's terrified expression as Jackson expertly nudged their car back onto the right side of the road in between two of the queuing vehicles, braking sharply as he did so.

She didn't need to look in the mirror to see what happened next; the squeal of tires and sounds of metal meeting metal at speed told her all she needed to know. She felt a flash of concern for the poor tourists who had crashed headlong into the black SUV before the surge of relief hit her that they had lost their tail — for now, at least. The other cars in the queue hit the brakes, and the car in front slid slightly as tyres fought for traction on the gritty road. Jackson again span the steering wheel so that they curved onto the opposite side of the road and around the car in one swift movement, barely tapping the brakes. Once clear of the obstructions, Jackson jammed a foot on to the accelerator and the car leapt forward, picking up speed and leaving the carnage behind them. Clara kept her eyes on the pile-up in the wing mirror until they rounded a bend in the road and a sheer rock face blocked her view.

'Do you think they are all right?' she asked, clenching her hands together to stop them from shaking.

'Hope not,' Jackson said with his eyes fixed firmly on the road ahead, flicking only occasionally to the rear-view mirror.

Clara stared at him. She knew what

he meant, of course. He hoped that the people tailing them were injured, or at least that their car was so damaged that they couldn't follow them, but all Clara could think about was the innocent people in the minivan. People, maybe a family on vacation, who had done nothing but be in the wrong place at the wrong time. She wondered who they would blame for the accident — but she knew who she blamed. All of this was her fault, and if someone was seriously injured back there — or maybe even dead — it was because of her.

She squeezed her eyes shut to try and block out the slow-motion replay of the accident in her head, but she couldn't. It came in waves, and no matter how hard she tried to focus on something else, it was there. The terrified look of the driver, the sound of broken metal . . . and she knew it was her imagination, but also the sound of terrified screams and people in pain.

'Hey.' Jackson's sharp word brought

her back to the car, and she opened her eyes, but the images continued to play as if on a cinema screen in front of her.

'Clara. Clara?' The second mention of her name was more urgent.

'Talk to me. What's going on? Are you hurt?' The concern in his voice made her blink, and for a moment at least the image subsided.

'I'm fine,' she said, although she knew she wasn't. All she wanted to do was curl up in a ball and cry until there was nothing left inside her, but she knew that she couldn't. The last thing Jackson need was a hysterical child losing it.

'No, no, you're not. Talk to me.'

Clara shook her head. She had nothing to say. Nothing that could sum up the last four days, all that she had seen, all that had happened because of who she was or because of who her father was.

The car started to slow noticeably.

'What are you doing?' she asked, slightly panicked.

'Checking you're OK,' he answered simply as he pulled the car into a layby opposite a viewing point. It was empty, but Clara could feel the danger behind them as if it was a ghostly presence.

'We can't stop!' she cried, her voice pitched higher than she intended. 'We have to get out of here!'

Hands reached over and pressed the button to release her seatbelt and she allowed herself to be pulled in to a one-armed embrace. She buried her head in his shirt and tried to take some breaths to calm herself. A gentle hand rubbed her back, and she expected Jackson to say something; but it was like he knew there was nothing he could say, and he just held her tight. The shakiness started to pass and her hands fell still in her lap. She took a deep breath and eased herself back in to her seat. She couldn't bring herself to look at him; she wasn't sure if it was because she was embarrassed at losing it, or if the sight of his concern would break down all the walls she was desperately trying to put up in her mind.

'I just need to fix something,' he said before sliding out of the car. Clara watched numbly as he fished something out of the trunk and there was the sound of an electric screwdriver. Eventually he climbed back into the car.

'Changed plates,' he said by way of explanation. 'We need to ditch this car soon but that will have to do for now.'

A few miles down the road and Jackson took a turning directing them to I-40. The signpost said 'Marion'.

'Aren't we going to Asheville?' Clara asked.

Jackson shook his head. 'We need to put some distance between us and whoever was following. They will, no doubt, have sent an update as to where we were. We need to get off the parkway and lose ourselves on the interstate.'

'But what about Asheville?' She wanted to add *What about Jessica?* but as much as she wanted to know the answer, she didn't think she could bear to cause him more pain.

'It's not safe. It may just have been bad luck that they found us, but . . . '

'Do you think Jessica . . . ?' She couldn't do it; she couldn't bring herself to finish the question.

'She may have been compromised.' Clara's breath caught in her chest, and the all-too-familiar ache of guilt was back: she had only considered the possibility that Jessica was part of it, that she had betrayed them. It had not crossed her mind that in helping them, she had put herself in danger, and maybe the worst kind.

Jackson was right about losing themselves on the interstate. Clara had no idea where they were: they seemed to travel a while and then head off on another road, before seemingly coming back on themselves. The sun had set many hours before, and Clara felt mesmerised by the oncoming headlights. Her head ached and her plastered arm felt heavy; she cradled it against her chest, trying to relieve the sense of pressure on her wrist.

For the first time in hours, she felt Jackson look at her. She didn't acknowledge his gaze, just kept staring out of the window.

'We'll stop at the next place. You need some rest — and, by the looks of you, some pain relief.'

'Don't worry about me. Just keep going.'

Again she could feel him study her, but she kept her eyes fixed ahead. She didn't know why, but she didn't want him to look at her or show her concern.

'We need to stop. I need to get a couple of hours' shuteye. Don't want to risk falling asleep at the wheel.'

Clara nodded her understanding but said nothing. Jackson was true to his word and pulled off at the next exit. The rest stop had a couple of low-rent motels, a 1950s-style diner and a pizza joint. Jackson pulled the car up at the first motel, parking in a corner away from the street lighting.

'Scoot down,' he said. 'I'll go sort us a room.'

Clara did as she was told, too tired and worn out to argue. She slid down in her seat but kept her eyes fixed on Jackson as he moved assuredly across the lot, scanning his surroundings all the while, before ducking in to the motel reception. Moments later and he was back, dangling a key in his hands.

'Take everything with you,' he said, grabbing bags out of the back. 'We won't be coming back to the car.'

He opened the door and ushered her inside before closing it quickly and pulling the chain-lock across. Clara stepped in, dumped her bags and headed straight to lie on the bed. She shut her eyes and willed sleep to come, but all she could see and hear were the events of the last few days. With her eyes closed, she forced herself to focus on what Jackson was doing: moving around the room, no doubt checking it out. A moment later a shadow passed over her eyelids and she opened her eyes. Jackson was crouched by the bed: in one hand he held a glass of water, and in the other a couple of small white pills. He offered them to her and despite her body's protests she sat up. Her hands shook as she took the pills, and Jackson steadied them with his so she could take a sip of water.

'Thank you,' she managed to say.

'It's going to be all right, Clara. Get some sleep.'

She shook her head. She wanted to believe him but she knew it wasn't true. It was never going to be all right. How many people had been injured or killed trying to protect her? What if Jackson was next?

'It's all my fault. Those people back there, and before that at the hospital, and back home . . . People I never even met have been hurt and worse trying to protect me.'

She felt Jackson move to sit next to her, and this time it was she who resisted. She had no right to ask for comfort and no right to receive it. She pulled away but he pulled her back, gentle but firm. And she was in his arms. He rocked her slowly and held her close. She could hear his heart beat in his chest, strong and slow.

'It's not your fault, Clara. None of this is your doing. You don't blame the victim of an assault, you blame the perpetrator. If you need to blame someone, blame them.'

She wanted to cry or to scream, to rail against the people that had turned her world upside down, but she couldn't. It was like she was empty all of a sudden, that they had taken everything from her and left her with nothing, not even herself. So she just let herself be held and allowed the darkness to overwhelm her.

17

Clara woke to the sounds of Jackson tossing the keys onto the small table. He dropped the paper bag of food beside them. Despite everything, Clara could feel her stomach rumble at the smell of fast food wafting from the bag. She pushed off the blanket that was covering her — presumably Jackson had been worried she would feel the cold — stretched to ease out the ache she felt all over, and walked over to the table. Jackson seemed immune to the potent smell, and instead was focused on taking a small gadget from its plastic wrapper. Clara quickly realised it was a telephone. For the first time in the last few days she thought about phoning her mum and stepdad. It wasn't that she had forgotten them — more like she hadn't allowed herself to think about them. Her feelings and concerns were pushed behind a high dam, and she knew that if she allowed them out she would not be able to function at all.

The desire to speak with them had been replaced by something stronger and fiercer — the need to protect them. She had seen enough people get hurt, and there was no way she would risk her family. She loved them too much, and for perhaps the first time she realised that sometimes love was about sacrifice, and if the recent events meant she could never go home, never see them again, then that was what she would do. Anything else would be pure selfishness.

Clara pulled one of the Formica chairs away from the table and sat down. Feeling inside the bag, she pulled out a breakfast burger and a small cup of coffee. She hadn't really been a coffee drinker before her trip to the US, but now she was beginning to develop a taste for it. The burger tasted amazing, and she had to keep herself from moaning her pleasure out loud. It was amazing how, when everything else had been taken away from you, junk food still tasted like the food of the gods.

'You enjoying that?' Jackson said with one eyebrow raised.

'Mmm,' was all Clara could manage. 'Why does junk food always taste so great?' She wiped a crumpled napkin across her chin to catch the drips of sauce that had spilled out.

'It's the chemicals the fast food giants put in it to make sure people keep coming back for more. It's why so many people are obese.'

Clara took the crumpled napkin and threw it at him. Outside, a car drove past, and its headlights illuminated the room for a few seconds. It was still dark outside, and the cheap clock on the wall told Clara it was four a.m.

'What are you doing? I thought we couldn't use phones,' Clara said as she washed her last mouthful down with coffee and tried not to think about the other burger lurking inside the bag begging her to eat it.

'Want to get on the net and find out

what's happening out there. Safest way is a burner phone. Brought it with cash so it can't be traced.'

Clara dragged her chair around the table so she could see over Jackson's shoulder as he brought up an internet news site. The headline read: 'No breakthrough on Senator's family kidnap drama.' Clara shivered: the thought of the small boy, terrified and alone, his poor family out of their minds with worry, was awful; and for a moment she wondered if her own family had any idea what had happened to her.

'Despite what the media like to think, just because they are reporting that there's been no movement doesn't mean there hasn't been.'

Clara stared at him. 'Do you think they've found him?'

Jackson shrugged. 'Could be. The best way to keep him and the rest of his family safe is to keep that fact secret.'

'But I thought you said that terrorists like to spread fear. Surely the sensible thing would be to tell the public that they had found him safe and well.'

'I'm just guessing here, Clara. It may be the headlines are right, but in a way the public probably feels safer if they think that the kidnappers still have a victim.'

Clara frowned.

'The public can be a bit sheep-like sometimes; they often feel what they are told to feel by the media or the government.' Jackson looked at her and she could feel his question. 'Cynical much?' she asked with a smile.

He shrugged again. 'Just my experience.' She saw a small smile form on his lips, only to be replaced by a hardness that made her withdraw just a little.

'What is it?' she asked, even though every part of her did not want to know the answer.

She watched as his thumb scrolled down through the page before he tossed the phone onto the table and stood up so abruptly that his chair fell backwards with a nerve-jarring crash. Clara jumped a little but reached out for the phone.

She forced herself to read the news story that had caused his outburst.

'Body of a woman found on Blue Ridge Parkway.'

Clara dropped the phone as if it had suddenly become super-heated. She tried to find her voice but she couldn't speak. She forced herself to pick up the phone again and read the rest of the story. She didn't make it to the end; bile rose in her throat, and it was all she could do to make it to the bathroom in time.

A hand offered her a glass of water and she took it, rinsing the sour taste from her mouth and then wiping her face on a towel. A hand carefully pulled her hair back off her face.

'You don't know it was her — Jessica — ' She forced herself to say the name even though it caused a stab of pain to run through her.

Jackson move from his crouched position to sit on the floor beside her, his back resting against the bathroom door jamb.

'It's her,' was all he said as he leaned his head back and stared at the ceiling.

Clara settled herself against the bathroom wall, her legs stretched out alongside Jackson's. 'I'm so sorry.' The words sounded empty to her ears, but what else could she say?

'It's the only explanation for why they found us so quick. If Jessica had betrayed me by choice, then we would have been nabbed before we got to Grandfather Mountain.'

They sat in silence side by side, close but not touching, both lost in their own thoughts. Clara didn't need to look at Jackson to sense his mood; he held himself tightly, and she knew that inside him there was a battle raging. She wanted to do something to take the pain away, or even to block it out for a few minutes, but there was nothing that she could think to say that didn't sound like lame platitudes.

Clara stared at the clock on the wall. Every tick reminded her of a second that was passing, perhaps bringing the inevitable closer, the moment that they would be found. She wasn't sure she cared anymore. Without waiting a moment, a moment that the sensible part of her brain could tell her to stop, she moved so that she was sat in Jackson's lap facing him, her knees folded each side of his legs. She expected him to lift her off, to tell her to stop, that he just didn't feel that way about her . . . but instead his eyes seemed to study her face. In those eyes she could see loss and pain, although his face remained blank. She reached up and ran her hand softly across his brow — furrowed slightly, the only sign of tension. His face seemed to relax a little as he leaned into her touch.

With her eyes locked on his, she leaned in and kissed him softly on the lips and felt him take a sharp breath. She didn't care in that moment if she felt more for him than he did for her. She didn't care if she would be another notch in his belt, another story of conquest to tell the boys over a beer.

She wanted to be with him, and their situation was so desperate that she didn't think she would get another chance.

His arms moved and Clara felt sure the moment was over, but instead he placed a hand on each side of her head and gently drew her to him. She allowed her lips to part as she felt his kiss become more urgent, needing his comforting touch as much as she felt he needed hers. Now she leaned in to him, feeling them press together, and a charge ran through her so that she shivered and, feeling the need to be even closer, pulled his body to hers.

His hands moved down the contours of her figure and she felt heat flash through her skin. She pulled back from the kiss and started to undo the buttons of his shirt. Her hands were shaking and she fumbled with the buttons as he lifted her top over her head. Clara shook out her hair and willed her hands to be still. As if he could read her mind, he tugged at his own shirt and pulled it over his head, losing a button in the process. Clara had the urge to laugh, but instead her lips found his again. She could feel his skin touching hers, hot, and when she dipped her head to his shoulder she could taste him. She felt his kisses move too as he worked his way around her jaw and down her neck. The jolts of electricity seemed to overload her brain and she felt a moan escape from her lips. Then she was moving in the air as he lifted her off of his lap and laid her gently on the floor. She arched her back in pleasure as his touch ran the full length of her torso to the waistband of her jeans, curving her spine so that he could remove the final barriers between them.

He rocked back on his heels so that he could slip off his cargo pants, and she moved with him, not wanting to be more than a finger-breadth away from him. Her eyes roamed his body, not sure where to look first. His physique was hard and trained and she wondered if she would ever be able to look at him again without this moment flashing through her brain on replay. Having shed this last layer he lifted her in his arms, as he had before, but this time was different. There was hunger and need and Clara knew that nothing else would quench her feelings at the moment. She wanted him; she wanted to forget all that had happened and to lose herself in him forever.

Clara's brain registered that neither of them had spoken, but she had no words to describe what she was feeling. She felt the bed beneath as he laid her gently down. His eyes drunk every inch of her in as hers had his. He moved to lay beside her and she turned so that she was facing him, slipping one leg over his hip to bring them together. His hand ran like burning fire from her hip to the back of her knee before he pulled her to him. Their lips met and Clara could feel Jackson's body respond as hers did with aching need.

'Clara,' he whispered softly into her shoulder as he nuzzled her neck. 'We shouldn't . . . I have no right.'

She lifted his face to hers. 'I don't care,' she murmured back. 'Right now I need to be with you, to be truly lost. Please . . . ' She was almost startled by the sound of her own desperation but it was all she needed to say. Strong hands at her back rolled her so that she was on top, and with one hand she pulled Jackson up so that they were entwined, facing each other. Her legs locked his body to hers, she could feel his legs drawing her in to him, and in that moment she knew they were both lost.

18

Clara felt cocooned, warm and safe, as if the outside world held no danger for her now. Strong arms held her close and she could feel the slow, steady heartbeat beneath the broad chest. Her eyelids closed slowly as she gave in to the feelings and felt comforting sleep drawing her back.

'We have to go,' Jackson whispered into her hair.

'Hmm,' Clara murmured. She felt Jackson shift his body, and she protested by trying to pull him back to her. He leaned in and kissed her on the top of her head.

'Clara, we have to go. It's not safe here.'

In one further swift movement she found herself alone in bed, and she watched as he worked his way around the room picking up his clothes and pulling them on. His movements were steady but she could feel the urgency in them. As much as she wanted to stay, to demand that he came back to bed, she knew that he was right. Words he had said a few days before played in her mind: that he couldn't protect her if he was distracted by even the hint of a relationship between them. She knew that she had pushed him at a weak moment, and although the memories of the intense pleasure and release were at the forefront of her mind, the nagging sense that she had endangered them both was finding its voice.

She rolled out of bed and grabbed at her clothes that Jackson had collected and laid out for her. Feeling slightly embarrassed, she turned her back to him as she slipped back into them. Jackson, for his part, busied himself packing up their limited possessions. Clara wasn't sure if he was reacting to her embarrassment or feeling his own. There was a part of her that desperately wanted to ask him what he was feeling, whether he was regretting giving in to her, but in another part of her didn't wanted to know. If she never asked him, she could preserve the memory as a perfect moment, one she doubted he would ever allow to happen again.

'What do we do now?' Clara asked, finally finding something sensible to say. She worked hard to keep her voice even, as if nothing had happened between them.

'We go to the only place that's safe.'

Clara looked at his face, which was set like stone as if all the feelings were locked away deep down. 'And where is that?' she asked, though she had a feeling she already knew the answer.

'The General's.'

★   ★   ★

Clara waited inside the motel room as she had been told, while Jackson went out to 'source a car'. She had wanted to ask what he meant, fairly sure that he wasn't planning to steal a vehicle since that would draw unwanted attention. A soft knocking at the door made her jump slightly, but she tentatively opened it with the security chain firmly in place. Jackson's face appeared, and without saying a word he indicated that she should follow him. She slipped the chain off the door and stepped outside. The sun was starting to rise and there was a dull light which seemed to muffle the noise of the diner opening for the early-bird customers. Clara followed Jackson as he made his way to an old, beaten-up-looking pick-up truck. It had obviously once been red, but had faded to a patchy pink in its many years of service.

Clara climbed in beside Jackson, who started the engine as if he were driving a truculent tractor and then he steered the pick-up out of the lot and rejoined the freeway. She tried to organise her thoughts so that she could work out how she felt about seeing the General again, but her mind refused to settle and she was distracted by images of her time with Jackson as they replayed, over and over. She shifted uncomfortably in her seat, hoping that Jackson wasn't able to pick up on her feelings.

'I know that you might not feel ready to see him again, but he really is the only person we can trust right now.'

Clara wasn't sure whether she was relieved that he hadn't guess the true reason for her distraction or hurt that he did not seem to be thinking about their time together at all. The pain was becoming all too familiar and she firmly reminded herself that she had known last night what she was doing, that she was an adult and she had been certain that she felt more for Jackson than he did for her. That she had decided last night that it was a risk she was willing to take, and that she had no right to feel sorry for herself this morning or to hold it against Jackson. She forced herself, with much effort, to focus on what could arguably be considered the more important matter in hand — her own safety, and that of Jackson, who she knew would risk his life to protect her own.

'I don't know how I feel about him,' she answered honestly, 'but I think you are right. He is the only person we can trust, so we don't have a choice. I'm sure we can both be grown-ups about our situation and the choices that were made.'

Jackson took a turning off the freeway heading north.

'So are we going back to Washington?' Clara asked.

He shook his head. 'No. We're heading out to a cabin the General uses for fishing when he occasionally takes a vacation.'

'That doesn't sound like a great idea. I mean, no offence, but won't that be one of the places that people will look for us, especially if they know the General as well as we suspect they do? Won't Agent Summers know to search there?' She hated mentioning his name; she didn't want to see the pain on Jackson's face, or to recall the memory of the man's word about Jackson's previous experiences with women.

'Trust me, Brad doesn't know about it. No one else does. The cabin has no paper or electronic trail that would lead someone to the General. Whenever he visits out there he follows an extensive avoid-and-evade program to ensure that no one can trace him.'

Clara had never considered that the General had had to live his life like that. She had always thought that sort of behaviour was only necessary for spies, and then probably only in the movies.

'He's been a high-profile target for many years, Clara. He has to live his life by very strict rules to protect himself and the nation.'

Clara tried not to roll her eyes at Jackson's overt patriotism. Somehow it made her uncomfortable — though whether that was because she wondered if he was telling her this to try and get her to go easy on the General, or because he truly believed it, she really wasn't sure.

'So how long will it take us to get there?' Clara said, needing to say something to steer the topic away from the General.

'Not sure.'

'But you know where we are going, right?'

He laughed. 'Roughly, yes.'

Clara took a moment to digest this. ''Roughly' as in you know which state it's in; or 'roughly' as in you know its exact coordinates?'

'We'll find it, but what I really meant is that it depends on how many detours we need to take, and how many times we need to swap vehicles.'

19

Clara felt sure that no one had been able to follow them. They had taken a dizzying number of detours and circular routes to the point that she had no idea if they had headed north or south or anywhere in between. There had been no stops for motels now; instead, Jackson had pulled the car over and catnapped for a few hours before heading back out onto the road. Since Clara had never been that great on just a couple of hours' rest, she had slept while they drove, which only added to her disorientation. Jackson seemed to be locked in his own world and resisted all her attempts to get him talking. She understood that he didn't want to speak about what had happened between them — it was a complication that neither of them were ready to deal with in their current predicament — but the silence was causing her frayed nerves to feel even more so, and she was beginning to feel like a kidnap victim herself.

The car slowed and Clara didn't bother to open her eyes. She figured that Jackson was in need of another power nap, and so she shifted slightly in her seat and willed sleep to come. Not easy in the cramped conditions: her back ached, and despite the jacket supporting her plastered arm, she couldn't get comfortable. She had tried to allow her mind to wander, to relax, but all she could think about was Jackson's touch on her skin and his closeness for that brief period of time. She wasn't sure why, but it embarrassed her, as if she was worried that he could read her thoughts.

'Stay here.' Jackson's voice jolted her from her latest romantic replay and she sat upright.

'Is something wrong?' Clara could feel her body tense, ready to fight or run.

'No. We're here. I'm going to go check it out.'

Clara could make out nothing in the blackness, not even shadows to give definition. In the silence she could just about make out Jackson's footfalls, and she marvelled at his ability to walk confidently in the pitch black, seemingly unconcerned about bumping into anything. She heard the creak of a wooden door open, and saw a small amount of light spilling forward. It was too bright for her eyes, and for a split second all she could see was dancing stars. The sound of murmured voices made her lean forward and peer through the windscreen. Jackson had said nothing about anyone else being here — she wondered if it was the General — and then the all-too-familiar fear was back: she could make out more than two voices.

Clara slipped across to the driver's seat and scrambled in the darkness for the keys in the ignition. They were gone. She cursed silently as she realised that Jackson must have taken them with him. The thought of Jackson made her pause. He had not shouted any kind of warning and there had been no sounds of a struggle. The many possibilities ran through her head: they had guns, they had killed or seriously injured him. But none of these seemed to explain his lack of warning; she felt sure he would have used his last breath to ensure she had at least a chance of getting away.

A chance of getting away. The thought paraded across her brain. Why hadn't he left her the keys to the car? On every previous occasion he had made sure she had the means to escape, without him if necessary. The fear deepened and she could feel an overwhelming heaviness in her heart. She tried to push it away, to force it back as some kind of nightmare scenario that couldn't be true, but the facts wouldn't let her. What if Jackson had betrayed her? What if he had been in on it all along and this was just some elaborate game to him? The fear was nudged aside by burning anger — at

Jackson, yes, but more at her own foolishness. She had surrendered herself to him like an inexperienced teenager. She let the anger flood her as she knew it was going to be a more useful emotion to her now than fear.

Keeping her eyes fixed on the glimmer of light from the building ahead, she reached for the car door handle and gently pushed. The noise of the door opening seemed as loud as a trumpet in the silence, but there was no movement from the cabin. She eased the door slowly outwards to allow a big enough crack for her to squeeze through. Once outside she dropped to a crouch, all the while studying the building. She pushed the car door to, but not closed, fearing a loud metal clunk. Awkwardly, she scrabbled around to the back of the car, trying to figure out the best direction to make a run for it. Part of her told herself that it was hopeless. She had no skills to rely on, and her enemies were likely to be highly trained soldiers or law enforcement officers — but there was no way she was going to give up without a fight.

She settled on heading back down the track to put as much distance between them and her as possible, and slowly rose from her crouch. A hand gripped her arm.

'Going somewhere, sweetcheeks?' The voice was familiar but the tone was not. She knew it was Jackson, but not *her* Jackson: not the strong yet gentle man who had somehow become her everything in those few short days. This was Jackson the soldier, hard and uncaring, with a job to be done.

'Let me go!' Clara hissed. 'What are you doing?'

Jackson laughed, harshly and without humour. Without saying a word, he dragged her towards the open door of the cabin. Inside, Clara could see that the light came from the fire and oil lamps set around the single room. There was very little furniture, just a single camping cot in the corner and a couple of fold-up chairs. A few rickety wooden cupboards stood at one wall, and Clara could see that the windows had been boarded up with rough planks, blocking out any light from the outside world.

There were people there, three men and a woman. One of the men — older than Jackson, with salt-and-pepper hair but a muscled body — leaned against the brick fireplace, and Clara knew instantly that he was in charge.

'I have to give you credit, Jack. You were right, it was worth the wait. The General's attention has been compromised, just as you said; and now . . . well, now he's got to be going out of his mind. His long-lost daughter and his most trusted lieutenant, fallen to the enemy.'

Clara glared at him but said nothing.

'I trust you had your usual fun, too,' Hollingsworth said as he walked towards Clara and lifted her chin up so he could study her. Clara fought the urge to spit in his face, but didn't want to give him the satisfaction of knowing that his comments had riled her.

'I look forward to a detailed report

when this matter is settled.' His voice was light with humour. 'Maybe over a beer?'

Clara wanted to scratch his eyes out, but she settled on slapping him hard across the face, wishing that Jackson had grabbed her other arm. She knew she could do more damage with her plastered arm, but allowed herself the satisfaction of watching the red streak grow across his face.

'Well, aren't you the fiery little cat,' Hollingsworth said, all trace of humour gone. 'Stubborn and willing to risk everything, just like your father. Lucky for you, we need you in one piece — for now.' The unspoken threat hung heavily in the air.

Clara tried to take a step back. The venom in the man's voice left her in no doubt of his intentions, but Jackson's grip was tight and she couldn't twist her body away.

Hollingsworth handed Jackson two pairs of cuffs which shone in the firelight. 'Stick her in the john. Make sure the cuffs are nice and tight.'

Jackson nodded before dragging Clara towards a door at the back of the room that she hadn't seen before. The room was tiny and smelt of water that had been still for too long. There was a low toilet bowl and a cracked, greying sink. Jackson shoved her and Clara found herself on the floor, narrowly missing crunching her head on the edge of the sink. She fought the urge to kick out at him, but instead let him cuff her good arm to the down-pipe from the sink and her right ankle to the fixings at the back of the toilet. Not only was she well and truly trapped, but her body was twisted uncomfortably and already sending her pain signals.

'Why are you doing this?' She knew she was wasting her breath but she had to ask. She needed to know for certain that he had betrayed her, that the Jackson she thought she knew was just an act or a figment of her imagination. Jackson shrugged carelessly.

'Why does anyone do anything? Money,

power, revenge. Pick your poison.' He checked the cuffs one last time and stood up before turning for the door. 'Watch yourself, Clara. Hollingsworth is as mean as a snake when he chooses.'

'What difference does it make? He's going to kill me anyway, isn't he?' Clara could feel her voice shake but she didn't care. What did it matter if Jackson knew she was terrified? He wasn't the man she had thought he was.

Jackson turned and looked her full in the face for the first time since they had left the motel. 'Yes, he is, but there are a thousand ways he can kill you. Behave, and he might make it quick.' His face showed no emotion at his words, and he turned and left without saying any more.

Clara couldn't breathe. However hard she tried, she couldn't force any air into her lungs. She had known she was going to die the moment she had realised that Jackson had betrayed her; but to have him, him of all people, confirm it seemed to make it all the more terrifying. She could feel tears prick at the edges of her eyes; the fear, the hurt and anger all welled up inside her, and she didn't bother to fight it. The nightmarish images of her mum and sister screaming and crying for help filled her vision. She felt as if she had lost everything that mattered, everything that she loved. Clara curled up in a ball as best she could and let it all out in hot, violent tears.

20

Clara wasn't sure how, but she had managed to cry herself to sleep. She woke to find her head and neck at a crooked angle, wedged under the sink. She lifted her arm to try and massage some of the tightness away, but her cuffed hand didn't have enough reach. She twisted herself around, moved her head towards her fixed arm, and did the best she could. She knew her neck would be more stiff and sore tomorrow but her mind casually told her it didn't matter since she probably wasn't going to be alive to experience it.

She marvelled at the new sense of calmness that she felt. Maybe she had given up; was accepting her fate. Or maybe it was something more? The fear was less, but the anger had been stoked. She wanted to fight, to hit out — and most of all, she wanted to live. She wanted to live long enough to tell Jackson what she thought of him. She wanted to live long enough to see him punished. She allowed the feelings to fill her up. Somehow, as she slept, her mind had accepted that it might all be over very soon; but if that was the case, then she was going to go down fighting. Perhaps she was more like her biological father than she had thought.

Clara edged towards the door, stretching her tied arm and leg to their very limits. Leaning in, she turned her head so that she could hear what was going on in the main cabin. At first all she could hear was murmuring, but she forced her mind to concentrate and the words started to make sense. The voices — Clara couldn't make out who was speaking — were discussing the best way to inform the General that he had failed to protect his daughter. There was laughter too, and Clara knew that they were just messing around, like it was some big joke. She felt sure they had a plan and that it would be meticulous. Every step of her journey with Jackson had probably been carefully planned. The thought of this made bile rise in Clara's throat, and for the first time she felt something for her father that wasn't a negative emotion. She felt something like concern: he had, after all, done his best to protect her, but been betrayed by the one man he had trusted above all others.

Another voice started to speak, louder than the others, and Clara recognised Hollingsworth's commanding tone.

'I need you to do this, Jack. Seeing you take an active part in all this will be a massive blow to him and his ego. The ultimate failure on his part, trusting you.'

Clara couldn't make out Jackson's response, but moved away from the door as she sensed that someone was walking towards it. She quickly settled back in to her original sleeping position and closed her eyes, willing her breath to become slow and steady as in sleep.

'Wakey-wakey, sweetcheeks.'

Clara ignored him and was rewarded

with a swift kick to her outstretched leg. She opened her eyes and glared. Jackson stood over her, and in the background, through the open door, she could see the others standing expectantly.

'What do you want?' Clara said.

'Why, you, of course, Clara. It's always been you.' Jackson's smile was cold and somehow sinister.

She inwardly grimaced at his words but kept her face smooth, simply raising one eyebrow in an unimpressed fashion. 'Are you going to kill me?' she asked, surprised at the lack of emotion in her own voice.

'Not before we share your capture with the General, no.'

If Clara hadn't known better, she would have said she could hear the old humour in his response; but his face told her different, set hard and cold.

Jackson knelt down and removed the cuff from her ankle before reaching over and unlocking her good wrist. He left this one in place and pulled on it to yank her to her feet. The lower half of her body was stiff and slow to respond, and she couldn't help but let out a yelp as the metal bit into her skin.

'Don't damage the goods, Jack. We can save that for later,' Hollingsworth said.

Jackson hooked his arm under her shoulder and pulled her to her feet. Before Clara could find her balance, she was being dragged out of the bathroom and into the main room of the cabin. In the centre of the room was a plain wooden chair, set facing the door. In front of the chair was a small video camera on a tripod. Jackson forced her to sit, cuffed her wrist to the back of the chair so her arm was pulled behind her, and then knelt down again and cuffed her ankle to the chair leg. Clara felt herself want to laugh — as if she was going to be able to undo one set of cuffs at her wrist, let alone two sets! The woman, who had said nothing until this point, stepped over and shoved a piece of paper in front of her eyes.

'Read this,' she said. Her accent was

vaguely American, but Clara couldn't place it. She looked up at the woman, and in that instant she knew what she was going to do.

'No,' Clara answered simply.

The woman took a step nearer and matter-of-factly grabbed a handful of Clara's hair and yanked her head backwards. Her face was so close that Clara could smell the coffee she had recently drunk.

'Read it or I will hurt you.' The voice was harsh but steady.

Clara blinked. The handfuls of hair were being pulled so tightly that she knew they were being torn completely from her head.

'No. You're going to kill me anyway, so why should I help you?'

The woman flashed her a sinister smile, like a cat about to take a mouse. 'Because we can make even death hard for you.'

Clara's brain managed to process the most important information from this statement. The sentence was unfamiliar, and the word order a little out. She had her first piece of information about this woman: she wasn't American, at least not originally.

The woman let go of her hair and Clara turned her face away, shaking her head slightly to try and relieve the pain. The woman held out the piece of paper again and this time Clara took it. The woman seemed satisfied and stepped away from Clara towards the camera. Taking instructions from someone behind Clara, she flipped open the screen of the video camera, and Clara watched as a red light appeared, telling her that the camera was rolling.

'Speak,' the woman said.

Clara glanced down at the paper, giving herself a few seconds to think. 'My name is Clara Radley. My father is General George Driscoll.' Clara paused. There was no way she was going to read out the rest, to plead for her father to do something to help her. She looked up and stared straight in to the camera. 'Dad.' Clara was surprised that her brain had found that word when thinking of the General. It was the first time she had used it out loud to describe him. Of course, it might well be the last time she had the opportunity to speak to him. Somehow, that thought gave her courage.

'Don't do anything they say; they're going to kill me anyway . . .'

Clara was cut off by an arm snaking around her neck and yanking her backwards.

'Turn it off!' Agent Hollingsworth's voice was quiet with steely rage. 'I thought you said she would do as she was told.'

Hollingsworth's voice was behind her, but she could tell it was not him who had her around the throat. 'She will,' Jackson said, his arm tightening slightly so that Clara could barely swallow.

'Read it, Clara,' he said, his voice rough with anger and frustration. 'I don't want to hurt you right now, but I will.' He leaned in, and Clara could feel his hot breath on her cheek. 'Trust me. Read it.'

Clara felt her body go limp as hope

surged through her. She didn't want to give in to it, knew that he was probably toying with her again, but it was a powerful thought: the smallest glimmer of hope. She tried to nod her agreement, but her head was held too tightly. After a moment's pause, the pressure was gone and Clara was able to look back at the camera.

'What did you say to her?' Hollingsworth said sounding both curious and amused.

'Just made a few suggestions of what she could expect next if she didn't.'

Clara heard rather than saw Hollingsworth clap Jackson on the shoulder. 'Well, it better work,' he said with a snort.

21

Clara did as she was told and dutifully read out the words typed on the piece of paper, Jackson's whispered words ringing in her head: *Trust me*. She didn't think she *should* trust him — the evidence against him was overwhelming — but the glimmer of hope was too powerful to ignore. She doubted it would make a difference, anyway; it seemed likely that her fate had been sealed days before. But she would go along with his plea, for now. She allowed some of the fear back in: if Jackson was telling the truth, then she needed the others to believe that whatever Jackson had said had frightened her into submission.

When she was finished, Hollingsworth watched the woman transfer the video onto a small laptop. He leaned over her shoulder as she replayed

Clara's speech, making small adjustments. Clara flinched at the sound of her own voice: she sounded younger than her twenty-six years, afraid and defeated. She felt a surge of guilt at the thought of the General watching it and seeing her so broken. Forcing the thought from her mind, she focused on those two words — *trust me* — letting the hope fill her up again.

'Stick her back in the bathroom,' Hollingsworth said, directing his comment to Jackson, who had been standing behind Clara, out of her line of vision.

'McKenzie and Hiaasen. You know what to do.' He threw a small memory stick to the man and the woman, who Clara saw nod before she was hoisted off of the chair and dragged back to the bathroom. Jackson dumped her unceremoniously on the floor and Clara could detect no sign, not even the smallest indication, that his words earlier had been true. She tried to comfort herself with the knowledge that

Jackson was a professional and would not risk a word of comfort to jeopardise the mission, even if she badly needed one in that moment.

Without saying a word, he shackled her to the sink down-pipe and the toilet, before stepping outside and closing the door. Clara could hear muffled voices again, but could not make out the words. The door opened again suddenly, and a hand threw in a bottle of water which landed in her lap. It was warm but as Clara struggled to remove the cap with her plastered hand she realised how thirsty she was. As the liquid hit her stomach, she was rewarded with a loud growl, and hunger also hit her — she couldn't remember the last time she had eaten. Having downed the entire bottle, she knew all she could do was wait. She had no skill in picking locks, and so no way to plan her escape, but what she *could* do was be ready for when Jackson made his move — if he made a move.

Clara had no idea how long she sat in the bathroom. The light faded quickly, but she knew the cabin was in a heavily forested area so that didn't give much indication of what time it was. The temperature seemed to drop sharply too and quickly she began to feel cold, which, along with her awkward position, was making sleep impossible. She shifted a small amount, trying to encourage the blood to flow back to her feet.

The sound of a chair being knocked over piqued her attention. She shifted again so that her head was nearer the door and she could hear better.

There were definite sounds of a struggle: crashing and the dull sound of fists hitting their mark. There were no voices, and so Clara could not tell who was winning in what was likely to be a fight between Jackson and Hollingsworth, unless someone else had come to join the party. She could hear footsteps approach the bathroom door and she drew back as far away from it as possible, hoping that it would be Jackson, rescuing her as always, proving her trust in him to be true.

The door swung open and Clara felt the pit of her stomach drop. Hollingsworth loomed over her, bleeding from a cut above his eye, and looking dishevelled but triumphant.

'You know the thing that really makes me smile, Clara?' he said as he roughly undid her cuffs and pulled her to her feet. 'The fact that Jackson actually thought I bought his routine. He really isn't that good an actor. And I know his type. If you cut them, they bleed in the colours of the stars and stripes.'

Clara's eyes took a few moments to adjust to the lamplight and she searched the room for signs of Jackson. 'He's over there, 'sweetcheeks',' Hollingsworth said lazily, indicating the far corner of the cabin.

She could make out a crumpled form lying on the floor. Her heart in her mouth, she focused on Jackson. He was lying on his back, taking ragged breaths, his eyes closed tightly, in obvious pain. She sagged, her legs stiff and tired, suddenly refusing to keep her upright. Hollingsworth, for his part, let her fall to her knees.

'You know he calls all of his conquests 'sweetcheeks', don't you? He's been under my command for many years. Great soldier. Even better agent, but he has one weakness — you can't trust him with the ladies.' Hollingsworth's eyes flashed with malice. 'There's no one to rescue you now, Clara. The General's received your message and he knows he's lost. And you know what that means.' He leaned down now and whispered in her ear. 'I've won.'

The fight in her was gone. She knew it was hopeless. She was alone, in a strange country, in the middle of nowhere. Her own family were on the other side of the ocean and she could only hope and pray that they were safe and protected. Jackson was hurt and if he didn't get help . . . Her mind couldn't form the thought or the words, but she knew that he couldn't help her anymore. Hollingsworth had taken everything from her: her life, her family, and now the man that she had come to love. A coldness welled upside her, icy fury pushing aside all other emotions. If it took her last breath she was going to ensure that Hollingsworth didn't get whatever it was that he wanted.

Hollingsworth was sat with his back to her, typing on the laptop. He had left her where she fell and seemed unconcerned about what she might be doing. Now was her chance; not much of one, but she was going to take it. Any opportunity to ruin his plans — even if only temporarily — she was going to take it.

Slowly, she moved so that her feet were underneath her. Ignoring the protests of her muscles, she forced herself to her hands and knees, gingerly bearing weight upon her plastered hand. The cuffs were gone now;

Hollingsworth obviously believed he didn't need to chain her up anymore. He seemed to think that he had broken her to the point that she would give up. Well, she was about to prove him wrong.

As quietly as she could, she got to her feet — swaying a little, but she gritted her teeth and focused on her balance. Hollingsworth continued to type, ignoring her. With her eyes she searched for a weapon. She knew that he would expect her to go and check on Jackson, maybe even to cry over his body — well, he was in for a surprise. The days spent with Jackson had taught her something: that when you have no choice, striking first is the only option. A few paces to her left were the remains of the chair she had been forced to sit on. It now looked as if it had been run over by a truck, but one leg had broken off fairly intact. Keeping her eyes fixed on the back of Hollingsworth's head, she bent down and picked it up in her good hand. The floor of the cabin creaked slightly, but Hollingsworth remained focused.

Clara stared at her feet before silently kicking off each of her trainers to reveal her bare feet. Stepping forward carefully, centring her weight on the middle of each floorboard she moved towards Hollingsworth's turned back. He was a highly trained professional, of course, so she didn't really expect him to be surprised as his hand thrust out and caught the downward swing of the chair leg. He pulled it roughly from her grasp and she fell forward onto her knees. He lifted his leg to kick her and she made her move. Grabbing hold of the foot as it swung towards her, she absorbed the force with a muffled 'Oof!' and then yanked as hard as she could.

22

Hollingsworth fell backwards against the table with the laptop, keeping his balance but momentarily distracted. Clara launched herself at him, thumbs seeking out and finding his eyes as her knee found its target between his legs. To Hollingsworth's credit, he merely grunted and then twisted her arm away, and Clara found herself face-down on the table with her good arm twisted painfully up her back. She tried to wriggle away, but his grip was certain and the movement only sent further pain shooting up into her shoulder.

'Nice try, but did you really think it'd work? Doesn't seem like you inherited your father's brains. Did you really think I could be surprised by an inexperienced girl-child like you?' He was leaning over her now and she could feel his harsh breath on her cheek. His weight was bearing down on her so she could barely take a breath into her lungs, and she wondered if this was it, if she had pushed him so far that he would kill her.

Then the pressure was gone as suddenly as it had started, and Clara slid to her knees. Twisting around, she watched in slow motion as Hollingsworth crumpled to the floor. Clara looked up and saw Jackson standing over him, swaying slightly. She took a gasping breath and then launched herself into his arms. He pulled her tight and she could hear his heart beating in his chest, a sound that she had thought she would never hear again. His grip was tight, but she could feel his balance falter and so she stepped back, each of her arms holding his as if she alone could keep his six-foot frame upright.

'Jackson?' she asked as her eyes sought for any signs of injury on his body. The dark spreading stain on his shirt confirmed her worst fears. Carefully she steered him to the nearby cot and made him sit.

'No time — we need to go. I don't know when the others will be back,' Jackson said, his voice surprisingly steady.

'We aren't going to get very far if you bleed to death,' she answered smartly as her fingers found the site where a knife had been forced into Jackson's abdomen. She swallowed down a wave of nausea. This was not the first battle injury she had seen, after all, and she gently explored the wound. She was rewarded with a hiss of pain from Jackson. 'It's not too deep, but we need to try and slow the bleeding. I don't suppose we have a first-aid kit?'

'I don't imagine it was on Hollingsworth's kit list,' Jackson said through clenched teeth.

An idea struck Clara. 'Bet there's one in the boot of the car. Do you have the keys?'

Jackson shook his head and nodded towards Hollingsworth. 'In his pocket. While you're there, you might want to cuff him,' he added, with the trace of a grin but breathing heavily.

Clara grabbed the cuffs from the floor of the bathroom and gingerly approached the prone form. She nudged him once with her foot, making sure to keep a safe distance, and when there was no movement she cuffed both his hands together and then his ankles. That would at the very least slow him down. He didn't look as if he would be going anywhere soon, as the blood flowed from a jagged wound at the back of his head.

She opened the cabin door a crack, checking that the coast was clear, and then made a run for the car. She cursed once as she dropped the keys from her shaking hands, but the image of Jackson bleeding made her concentrate. She opened the boot of the car and found a small first-aid kit in one of the side pockets. Grabbing it, she ran back to the cabin.

'Take a roll of bandage and push it hard into the wound,' Jackson said.

Clara lifted an eyebrow. 'I've done

this before, you know. You'd be surprised how much patching up I've had to do on my travels.'

She tore the plastic wrapping from the small roll of bandage with her teeth and then pushed it firmly into the wound. Jackson's body stiffened in pain and when she looked up she could see the sweat pooling at his hairline. Taking a deep breath, she pushed on the bandage one more time and the bleeding seemed to slow. Reaching into the first-aid kit she pulled out a larger bandage and quickly wrapped this tightly around Jackson's abdomen. She placed her hand over the site of the wound and pressed down firmly with both hands, willing the bleeding to stop. She could feel Jackson's eyes studying her, but she focused on the job in hand.

'I'm sorry for the ruse, but it was necessary.'

She looked at him then, and forced herself to smile. 'I know. I mean, I understand.' And she did. He was, as always, just trying to save her life; but she didn't think she could put into words the feeling of betrayal, even if it had only been temporary. She looked away and focused again on stopping the bleeding.

'We need to go, Clara. The others could be back any time and we need to get out of here.'

She nodded and helped him to his feet. Slipping herself under one of his shoulders, she supported him to the door. 'OK. But this time I'm driving.'

23

Clara put the car into drive and sped off down the track. The car bounced as she navigated the deep ruts formed by the recent rain, and she could sense rather than see Jackson wince in pain. She forced her adrenaline-addled brain to focus, and slowed down. If she crashed the car or went off the track they would really be in trouble. It was dark, with the moon well hidden by the clouds, and Clara kept just the side lights on, which were enough for her to see a couple of feet in front and might give them a few seconds' warning before another vehicle saw them — specifically Hollingsworth's people, who she felt sure would be returning soon.

'So, fill me in,' Clara said. Now she had slowed the car from breakneck speed to merely fast, she felt sure she could manage a conversation.

'Hollingsworth is a traitor,' Jackson answered.

Clara rolled her eyes. 'You know what? I had kind of figured that out all by myself with all the threats. Who is he?'

'He's my boss. Senior special agent, in charge of my team within Army intelligence. He's an old friend of your father's. I had some concerns, but I didn't want to accuse him without evidence.'

'Please tell me we didn't go all through this, including you getting stabbed — ' Clara's eyes briefly checked out his wound before she refocused on the road. ' — just to prove what you suspected.'

'He was my mentor, Clara. I've trusted him with my life more times than I can count. I had my suspicions, but I wasn't prepared to ruin the man's reputation and career over unsubstantiated information.' Jackson turned his head away from her to stare out of the window, though what he could see in the darkness, Clara wasn't sure.

Her mind was racing again. He had put her in danger to discover the truth, and she wasn't completely sure how she felt about that. She wondered if her father had agreed to that part of the plan, but she didn't know him well enough to decide. She could understand the level of loyalty that both Jackson and her father felt — it was something that she looked for in her own friends and family — but it was also one of the many reasons that she found the General's approach to fatherhood so deeply painful. It was bizarre how a trait she felt attractive and on her 'must have' list for a man could leave her feeling so torn.

'So this was an actual plan.' She waved one hand around vaguely.

'Well, not all of it, obviously.'

Clara looked at him, hoping to see the familiar grin, and was rewarded. She couldn't help but laugh. Their situation was dire, and yet the sight of a genuine grin from him was enough to set right all the previous wrongs.

'So what was the plan?' she asked. 'I need specifics.'

'I told the General that I had suspicions about individuals close to him and to me. Five individuals. I didn't name anyone and he accepted that. He agreed to allow me to test my theory as long as I could keep you safe.'

Clara nodded, but she could feel him shift uncomfortably in the seat beside her. 'How's the pain?'

'Manageable. That's not the problem, Clara. I failed you and your father.'

Clara snorted. 'Hardly! You're the reason that I am still breathing, remember, and I don't think the General is going to complain too much when he sees what it has cost you.'

'Getting injured is part of the job, Clara. We train for that, we train to put our lives on the line for others. What we don't accept is failure.'

'But you haven't failed!' She could feel herself getting angry now. 'We both made it out. We just need to get you to a hospital for some proper treatment, then we can contact the General and get him to pick up Hollingsworth and the others.'

'It's not as simple as that. They're terrorists and they function like them. They have individual cells, who have no knowledge of the work of the other cells. They are completely separate and independent. We have caught one cell, the cell that was targeting you, but there are others.'

Clara took a moment to digest this. 'The people who took the Senator's nephew?'

Jackson nodded. 'Hollingsworth may know more, but he's highly trained and won't reveal any information.'

The track had reached a hard road surface, and Clara figured they were heading back towards civilisation. 'Which way to the nearest hospital?' she asked.

'Left, but I need you to go right.'

Clara determinedly steered the car to the left.

'I know we drive on different sides of the road, Clara, but you turned left.'

'Hospital is our number-one priority,' she said firmly.

'Actually, it's not.'

'What's more important right now than getting you emergency care before you bleed to death?'

'I think I know where he is.'

Clara frowned. 'I know where he is too, Jackson. We left him trussed up like a chicken back at the cabin, remember?' She was wondering if the blood loss was starting to affect Jackson's mind.

'Not Hollingsworth, Clara. I think I know where Daniel Robinson is.'

Clara kept her face forward concentrating on the road ahead. 'How do you know?' she asked.

'Something I saw on Hollingsworth's computer. The thing with cells is that they don't need to know what the others are doing, but someone has to be coordinating it all. When I saw Hollingsworth at the cabin, I knew that even if he wasn't in charge, he'd know more about what was going on than any of the others.'

'Then we have to get a message to

the General. He can do whatever he does and send some people to rescue him.' Clara waited for Jackson to agree with her, to tell her what his new plan was, but there was nothing but silence. She risked a glance, wondering if he had passed out.

'There's no time, Clara. They intend to kill the boy, whatever happens. That much seems obvious now. We can't get a message safely to the General without being concerned it'd be compromised. We have no way of knowing who's involved and who we can trust.'

Clara took a moment to digest this latest piece of information. She had thought the nightmare was finally over, that she could drive Jackson to the nearest hospital to get him treatment, and then ring her mum. Finally, she could speak to her family and check that they were safe too. She had played out the imaginary phone call in her head so many times she almost believed that she had already spoken to them. But she knew this was not an option. If they were, as Jackson suggested, the boy's only hope of rescue, there was no way that she was going to turn her back on a poor kid who was even more of an innocent victim than she herself was.

'So what are we going to do?'

'We aren't going to do anything, Clara. I'm going to get the boy, but before that I'm going to find you somewhere safe to hide.'

'No deal,' Clara said.

'I wasn't trying to make a deal, Clara, just stating the facts.' His voice had switched to hard, measured and professional.

'OK,' Clara said, 'let's examine the facts. If you were fighting fit, I'd probably agree with you. The boy's best chance would lie with you. But you aren't. You're hurt, and however happy you are to die the hero, I doubt Daniel Robinson or his family would feel the same. So the facts are that in your current state you need help, and I'm it.' She fought the urge to fill the silence with more words. She knew she had made her point and had nothing else to add, but she was desperate to convince him. There was no way she was going to let him risk his life again in a vain effort to keep her safe.

'I can't let you do that, Clara. I can't. It's probably a trap. Hollingsworth is a careful man — he has to be in his line of work — and the information on his computer was likely a test to see if I really had gone over to his side.'

'OK, it might be a trap, but it doesn't seem like we have much of a choice. If you're worried, I can tell the General that I made you take me or something.'

'You think the reason I don't want you to come is because I am worried about what the General will think?'

Clara could feel her heart beating in her chest and she tightened her grip on the steering wheel. 'Well, isn't it?' she answered finally, in a small voice.

A hand reached over and she felt it gently lift hers from the wheel. 'Clara. I don't want you to come because I don't want you to get hurt, any more than you already have. It's not about the General, it's about you.'

Clara pulled the car onto the dirt shoulder. However much time pressure they were under, this was a conversation that she needed to have with Jackson face-to-face. 'So this is about me?' she asked.

'Yes. It wasn't at first, but now . . . ' He lifted a hand to her face. 'I won't let anything happen to you. I couldn't live with myself.'

Those were the words that Clara had been longing to hear since their night together, and she could feel tears of relief pricking at her eyes as she tried to process her emotions. Jackson smiled; he had never met a woman like her. She was so refreshingly different, so honest and open. He had known that he might only have one chance to tell her the truth, to say out loud what he was feeling, and so he had said it. All other thoughts and concerns were pushed aside for one moment of honesty, which he hoped would convince her that he was right, she had to stay out of this.

'Then you have to know that I feel that way too,' she said, looking at him and studying his face.

'I do.'

'Then you know why I have to come with you.'

'Clara . . . '

She held up her hand. 'I love you, Jackson Henry, and there is no way that I am letting you go off on a suicide mission. Not when I could help.'

'I know you want to help, but you can't, Clara. If you're there, I'll be more worried about you than anything. Face it, sweetcheeks, you're very distracting.'

'Then let's use that to our advantage,' she said with a raised eyebrow. 'Now tell me where we're going.'

24

'This is not a plan; it doesn't even have the right to be called a plan,' Jackson said, shaking his head.

'If you've got any better ideas, then I'm all ears.'

'I do, actually. You drop me off, then head for the nearest motel, and I go get the kid.'

'That's not a better idea, that's voluntary stupidity. Look, you said it yourself — I'm a distraction. They know who I am, right? I mean, they know what I look like.'

'Yeah, but offering yourself up as a sacrificial lamb is not that far from voluntary stupidity.' Jackson winced as he manoeuvred himself out of the car. Clara put out a hand to steady him.

'So I distract them by knocking on the door, which they won't expect, and you go round the back and get Daniel.'

'You realise that you plan is based on trained professionals being surprised by an unexpected face knocking on the door of a secret location?'

Clara rolled her eyes. 'You said it yourself: they're hiding in plain view in an average suburban street. The only reason they haven't been noticed so far is that they have kept a low profile. All I have to do is get their attention, and then you do your thing.' Clara waved her hands in a vague manner; she could feel Jackson staring at her incredulously.

'OK, so what would *your* plan be? It's not like we have time to plan the D-Day landings, is it?' Clara had her hands on her hips, and for a moment she had a flash of how completely out there her life had become.

'I was going to sneak around back, take out the guards and rescue the kid.'

'Right, so me distracting them at the front door wouldn't help at all?'

'Not if I am worried about you, no.'

'Well, stop worrying, bucko; they're

hardly going to shoot me on sight. It'd kind of give it all away to the neighbours.'

Clara went to move away, but Jackson grabbed her arm.

'It's not a game, Clara.' His words were firm but uncritical. 'These people are trained killers. They were chosen because they have no qualms about killing a ten-year-old boy. They won't hesitate to hurt you if you get in their way.'

Clara placed her hand on top of Jackson's and gently lifted it off. 'I know. The last week has pretty much been out of a bad action movie. But we don't have a choice, unless you've come up with a plan to call the local cops.'

Jackson shook his head. 'First sign of trouble and the kid's time is up.'

'Exactly. So let's just do this.' Clara put a hand on either side of his face. 'And be careful. We have a conversation to finish, and I can't have it on my own.' She pulled his face towards her and brushed her lips against his. She wanted to kiss him properly but refused to let her mind dwell on the fact it could be the last time. There would be plenty of time for kissing later, when all this was over.

'A conversation?' Jackson looked momentarily confused, but as soon as the expression appeared it was gone, to be replaced by what Clara now thought of as his 'business' face. She rolled her eyes. *Men!*

'Don't hang around, and don't let them get you inside the house.'

'I know. You've told me several times.'

'I mean it, Clara. Whatever happens, do not step inside that house. The plan is to distract them and then get out of there. Understand?'

'I understand,' Clara said, though she knew deep down that if anything went wrong, she wouldn't be able to keep her promise.

As she walked away, she could feel Jackson's gaze on her back, so she forced herself to put confidence into her step. She told herself that all she had to do was walk up to the front door and knock on it. Nothing to it. But she knew that this was unlikely to be the case. Jackson was right, these were trained professionals who were impossible to surprise and would have reaction times that far outstripped her own. She also knew that she had no choice. There was no way she was going to leave a ten-year-old boy to his fate while she hid out in a motel room. There was also no way she was going to let Jackson, injured as he was, take all the risk.

She knew she shouldn't, but she cast a glance over her shoulder. The car was parked and there was no sign of Jackson, he was gone. The fear that she would never see him again threatened to overwhelm her, and she felt her throat and chest constrict with the pain. She stopped for a moment, on the sidewalk but out of view of the house, and allowed herself a few moments to compose herself. The only way she was going to see Jackson alive again was if she could cause enough of a distraction to force the men into a misstep, and she was going to do it.

She walked up the driveway with her good hand in her pocket, tightly clenched, and her plastered hand behind her back. The car parked on the drive was a typical nondescript family model, similar to all the other vehicles in the family neighbourhood. The front lawn was manicured and the borders revealed that a gardener was employed on a regular basis. There was nothing on the outside to give the slightest hint of what was going on inside. The driveway led to a path which crossed the front of the house. The blinds were partially closed but Clara knew that she was being watched, she could sense it. She turned her head away, hoping that she would not be recognised — the surprise needed to be when she was on the front doorstep.

The house had a double-wide front door, made of heavy wood, and to one side there was an old-fashioned bell-pull. She knew that the people in the house would already be aware she was there, but decided to pull it anyway. The sound seemed to reverberate around the house and Clara wondered how the owners of the property put up with it. The door opened surprisingly quickly, and Clara blinked in surprise as she was faced with a young woman of about her own age, the very image of the stereotypical soccer mom. The woman smiled and Clara managed to work her face into a smile in return.

'Hello,' the woman said brightly. When Clara did nothing but stare, the woman's smile dropped slightly. 'Can I help you?'

Clara's mind was racing. She wondered if Jackson had been right — not about the trap, but about the validity of the information. Had Hollingsworth set them up? Had he allowed Jackson to access information because it was all part of the plan? A coldness passed through her at the thought that Daniel was not here, and her mind froze as it tried to process the feeling of failure.

'Are you OK? You don't look well, why don't you step inside? I can make you a drink?'

Clara shook her head. She couldn't seem to find her voice. The woman stepped over the threshold and placed a hand on her arm.

'Really, you look awful. Come in for a minute. Maybe I can help.'

Clara tried to take a step back but the pressure on her arm increased. 'Step inside now, Miss Radley.' The pitch and tone of the voice were in keeping with the image of the friendly soccer mom, but the meaning was not lost on Clara. She tensed. It was a trap! She readied herself to make a run for it, trying to work out which direction she should run in.

'I wouldn't if I were you. We have the boy and your boyfriend, Miss Radley. No harm will come to them if you just step inside without a fuss.'

Jackson's words echoed around her head: *Don't let them get you inside the house.*

25

'I will count to three, Miss Radley. I wouldn't test me if I were you.'

Clara was left in no doubt of this, and she forced herself to take a step forward. The woman followed her in and closed the door behind them, pushing the deadbolt across. With a push, Clara was directed to walk towards the stairs and through a door which led down into the cellar. It was dimly lit by a single lightbulb and Clara nearly missed her footing. She desperately scanned her surroundings for signs of either Daniel or Jackson. She stepped off the last stair and could make out a small camp bed in one corner. The rest of the cellar was as she had imagined, full of various items that had no place in the house: several old bikes, piles of cardboard boxes, and a lawnmower. The woman gave her another push and indicated that Clara should sit.

'Daniel, you can come out now. I've brought you a friend to keep you company.' The voice was sneering now, and Clara knew for certain that her initial assessment had been entirely wrong. This woman was no soccer mom, and was not troubled by a conscience in any way. The door slammed and then the dim light was gone with the flick of a switch. Clara was left in darkness. There was a noise to her right and she turned her head, blinking, to try and make out what it was. She was suddenly dazzled by a light and threw her plastered hand in front of her face, remembering just in time to avoid giving herself another nosebleed.

'Daniel?' she said softly, not wanting to scare him any further.

'Who are you?' a young voice said, the light in her face unwavering.

'My name is Clara, Daniel. I came to try and help you.'

'By getting locked in the cellar with me?' The light lowered a little and Clara could make out a small shadow behind what she could now see was a torch.

Clara managed a smile. 'It wasn't exactly part of the plan,' she admitted, 'but I didn't come alone. Have you seen anyone else?'

'There's that woman, the man calls her Beth. She's mean, I don't like her.' Clara felt the camp bed give a little as Daniel sat beside her.

'She reminds me of a teacher I had at school,' Clara said. 'We called her Mrs Grotbags.' She was rewarded with a small giggle. Clara held out her hand, having decided that Daniel might not want a hug. Daniel looked at her hand and then took it, giving it a shake.

'The man — is he mean, too?' Clara asked, hoping that Daniel knew something about Jackson. Daniel shrugged.

'He's OK. He got me some chips and comics. He tells Grotbags . . . ' Daniel shifted besides her, pulling his knees up and resting his chin. ' . . . to leave the light on, but she always turns it off.'

'That's pretty mean. Where did you get the torch — I mean flashlight?'

'Found it,' Daniel said proudly. 'One of the boxes has camping stuff in it. I don't leave it on all the time. My dad says it's important to save batteries . . . ' His voice trailed off and Clara put an arm around his shoulders, pulling him into a one-armed hug.

'Your dad is looking for you, everyone is. They are going to be so impressed by how brave you've been.' Daniel sniffed, but to Clara's relief didn't pull away.

'Did they take you too?'

Clara gave him a squeeze. 'They tried to, but a man named Jackson stopped them.'

'Is he here too?'

'Uh-huh,' Clara said, swallowing the lump in her throat. 'He pretty much rescues people for a living. I mean, that's his job.'

'Like Superman?'

'Yep, just like Superman.'

Clara closed her eyes and refused to allow her imagination to run wild. She couldn't even know for sure that Jackson had been captured. For all she knew, he had managed to escape and was coming up with a new plan, one to rescue both her and Daniel. One that meant they could all go home.

'Someone's coming,' a small voice whispered in Clara's ear. She opened her eyes but stayed completely still, apart from giving Daniel's hand a squeeze. There were sounds of the door opening, and light spilled down the wooden staircase, causing Clara to turn her head away from the glare.

'Get up here,' the woman's voice sounded. 'Both of you — now.'

Clara slipped her feet to the floor and tried to stand up, but Daniel was clinging to her and his weight prevented her from moving.

'It's OK. We'll stick together and we'll be OK.' Clara reached for Daniel's hand and he shakily stood beside her, leaning into her. Clara moved her hand around his shoulders.

'I'm scared,' he whispered.

'Me too. But we aren't going to let Grotbags see that, are we?'

Daniel's face showed the glimmer of something other than fear, and Clara knew that was all she could do for now. She was more determined than ever to get him safely home. Clara led the way up the stairs and stepped out into the hallway of the house.

'Kitchen,' Beth said, gesturing her head. Clara walked forward with Daniel close besides her.

'Not the kid.' Clara felt Daniel's hand tighten in hers.

'He's scared. Let him stay with me, please,' Clara said.

'Of course,' Beth said, transforming back into soccer mom mode. Daniel relaxed a little, but Clara knew sarcasm when she heard it.

'What difference does it make?' Clara asked softly. 'He's just a kid. He's been through enough already.'

Beth leaned in so close that Clara

could feel her harsh breath on her cheek. 'You're right, he has, and I'm thinking that he probably doesn't need to see what is going to happen to you and loverboy before he goes night-nights himself.'

Clara swallowed bile and fought the urge to strike out. If she had been by herself, she might have risked it — after all, her future seemed to be cast in stone — but while Daniel was here with her and there was a chance, however small, that he might make it through this, she knew she couldn't. Holding on to Daniel's hand, she knelt down before him.

'I need you to do as you're told,' she said, wiping a smudge of mud from the boy's pale and drawn face. Daniel shook his head vigorously.

'Please Daniel, I promise it will be OK.' She forced the words out even though she knew that she would in all likelihood not be able to keep her promise.

'Remember Superman.' Clara risked

a glance, but Beth just looked bored and impatient. Daniel nodded slowly, and for a moment Clara wasn't sure he was going to let her go, but his small hand slipped from hers and he allowed himself to be taken away into the lounge. Clara watched as Beth gave him a shove. She heard a soft thud and knew that the force had been too great and that Daniel had fallen. She made to rush forward but a glare from Beth stopped her in her tracks, and all she could do was watch as Beth turned a key in the door. Clara strained her ears for any sound of Daniel's, but could hear nothing. All she could do was hope that he was OK.

26

Beth jerked her head in the direction of the kitchen door, which was closed, and Clara put a hand forward to open it. She pushed the door open and walked into the large room. In the middle was a central island, and a man was sat on a barstool with a wad of gauze to his head. He didn't need to turn for Clara to know who it was. Without looking around, he slid off the barstool and walked to the far end of the kitchen. Clara's eyes followed him, and she had to hold in a gasp at what she saw. Jackson lay on the tiled floor, still and pale.

'*Déjà vu*. Don't you think so, Clara? I mean, we've been here before, haven't we? Bravery to the point of stupidity, both of you. You could have got away home free, but no, you had to come and try and rescue the boy.'

Clara said nothing, just continued to stare at Jackson's prone form, looking for any signs of movement. Seeing her gaze, Hollingsworth drew back a foot and kicked Jackson hard in the gut. Jackson groaned and Clara tried not to sigh with relief.

'Leave him alone,' she said defiantly.

'You have yet to realise, Miss Radley, that no one around here is going to do as you ask. You might be the illegitimate child of a General, but you are not him.' Hollingsworth held her gaze as he casually stood on Jackson's right hand. Clara tried to run forward but Beth caught her by the hair and pulled her back.

'Let her go,' Hollingsworth said in a manner that suggested he was bored with his game. 'Let them have a few last moments together.'

The pressure on Clara's hair slowly lessened, and with a shake of her head she ran forward, falling to her knees by Jackson's side. She reached out a shaky hand to his face, almost afraid to touch him.

'Great plan, sweetcheeks, great plan.'

Clara let out a hiccupping sob as Jackson opened his eyes and looked at her. His smile was tight and his breathing laboured, but she was so relieved to see him she had to restrain herself from falling into his arms.

'Switch on the news channel. We are nearing the Senators' vote,' Hollingsworth's voice sounded. 'Then maybe you could have a go at fixing my head. I need to look my best for later.'

Clara ignored them, focusing only on Jackson. Gently, she lifted his shirt, and winced as she saw that the bandage was soaked through with fresh blood. Reaching up, she grabbed a tea-towel which was hanging on the end of the bench; she risked a glance over her shoulder, but either Hollingsworth hadn't seen her or didn't care. Carefully, she pulled off the soaked gauze that covered the wound and pressed the tea-towel down hard. She felt Jackson's body go rigid with pain.

'Sorry,' she whispered.

'S'OK,' he whispered back through clenched teeth.

'Daniel's here,' she said, trying to keep her hands from shaking. She was so relieved to see him again, but so afraid of what would happen next, and the emotions seemed to be waging a battle inside her. Jackson twisted, and with heavy breathing forced himself to sit up with his back resting against the end of the bench.

'Is he OK?' Jackson said, moving his head so he could see the television which was integrated within the central island.

'Scared, but they haven't hurt him. Grotbags has locked him in the front room.'

Jackson raised an eyebrow. 'Grotbags?'

'Beth, or whatever her name is. She reminds me of a teacher I had at primary school,' Clara said, with what she hoped was a nonchalant shrug; she couldn't believe this was what they were talking about, when who knew how much time they had left?

'And now back to the Senate, with the crucial vote reaching its final stages.' The suave newscaster's voice carried across the kitchen.

'What do you think he will do? The Senator, I mean,' Clara asked Jackson.

'If he has any sense, he will do as he's told,' Hollingsworth said from his barstool. Beth was working with a cloth and some strong-smelling antiseptic on the deep gash across the back of his head. To his credit, he didn't show any signs of discomfort as she dabbed the cloth on the wound.

'Why should he? You're going to kill Daniel anyway, aren't you? Maybe he's figured that out. Maybe you won't get what you want after all,' Clara said loudly.

Hollingsworth laughed harshly and Beth gave her a contemptuous stare.

'I don't care which way he votes, 'sweetcheeks'. He could vote for Kermit the Frog to run for president for all I care. I get paid either way.'

Beth gave him a frosty glare.

'Sorry, *we* get paid whatever happens, as long as we complete our task.'

'So you *are* going to kill him,' Clara said. 'He's just a kid — what has he done to you?'

'Well, right now he stands between me and twenty-five million dollars, so I think I can be forgiven for being keen to 'remove' him from my path.'

'And us?' Clara didn't want to know the answer but somehow she had to ask.

'You two? Well, you're just an added bonus. Once the Senator has cast his vote, we get rid of the boy, and then we have some quality time together before I have to go and get my money.'

'You're going to kill us,' Clara said.

'Eventually,' Hollingsworth replied. 'Now, shut your trap. I may not care how he votes, but I want to see what he looks like when he does, poor bastard.'

27

The inevitability of her situation hit Clara as hard as if she had been punched in the stomach, but after a moment of overwhelming fear, it receded and she felt a sense of calmness fill her. If she did nothing, she was going to die — of that much, she was certain — and the manner of her death was not something she wanted to think about. If this was it, truly it, then she had nothing to lose, but perhaps her death could mean something. Perhaps she might be able to save Daniel.

'I know that look, Clara,' Jackson said, the warning tone back in his voice. 'Whatever it is, forget it.'

Clara forced herself to look him square in the eye and swallow down the wave of pain at the thought of losing him. She had never really allowed herself to consider that they might have a future together, but she also knew that she had never felt like this about anyone else before. She loved him; of that, she was certain.

'We're going to die so we may as well go out fighting.' She frowned at him, wondering what he was thinking. He had told her that failure was worse than death, so surely he would agree to her plan, however crazy it might be.

'Don't give up on us yet, sweet-cheeks.'

Clara kept her face carefully neutral, knowing that any sign of a reaction might give something away, although she had no idea what that something might be. She leaned forwarded and lifted the front of Jackson's shirt to check her makeshift bandage.

'You have a plan?' she whispered, paying close attention to the small amount of blood that had seeped through to the tea-towel. At least the bleeding had slowed, she thought, even if it had not stopped altogether. She looked up at Jackson; his face was pale and tight, and there was a sheen to his face which told her that she needed to do something or Jackson would be lost to her forever. She also knew it was quite possible that would happen before Hollingsworth had a chance to end his life.

'Well, whatever it is, you're in no fit state to do anything heroic.' She tried to resist the urge but couldn't so lifted her hand to his cheek.

'Looks can be deceiving,' Jackson said with a small shrug. Clara rewarded him with a low snort.

'Are you trying to tell me that this is a fake wound? That you're not really lying on this kitchen floor bleeding out?'

'No, that much is definitely true.' He added a wince for good measure as he tried to move slightly. He reached out for Clara's hand and gave it a squeeze.

'We're not alone, Clara.'

She stared at him, wanting to ask him, desperate to know more, but she knew the risks. Her curiosity could ruin everything, and it wasn't just her life at stake. She nodded her understanding and held her tongue. Jackson raised an eyebrow in mock surprise and she had to fight the urge to thump him. Instead, she shifted around and sat beside him, leaning in and feeling Jackson place an arm around her shoulder. She felt a sense of hope grow and she allowed it to push away the fear and sadness.

'Don't let him fool you, Miss Radley. I've seen him cuddle up to more than his fair share of damsels in distress. It's a shame, really, that you are going to get to see what happens after. When you find that the life you have been secretly planning together in your head is nothing but a childish fantasy. He would walk away without so much as swapping phone numbers or a promise to call — not that he'll get the chance this time.' Hollingsworth tore his eyes away from the screen for a moment. His face was amused, as if he enjoyed inflicting pain on others — which Clara suspected was true, and for a moment she wondered that Jackson and this man had ever been friends. The very thought caused doubt to rise in her mind again, but she shoved it back. Jackson was loyal and trusting, and he had told her himself that he would remain so until there was clear evidence to the contrary. That evidence could not have been clearer if it had been written in the sky.

'I'm sorry,' she said, turning to Jackson, wondering what he must be feeling to have been so betrayed by this man who he considered to be a father figure.

'For what? Getting me into this mess? That's not your fault, Clara, none of this is; and besides, I've gotten myself into plenty of trouble before I met you.'

'And no doubt there is more trouble to come.'

She felt him turn his head and kiss her gently on her temple. 'That's my life, sweetcheeks. Trouble tends to follow me around in this job.'

'But you don't normally get stabbed by your mentor.'

'Well, that's a first,' he admitted.

Clara wanted to reply, to say something comforting, but she could think of nothing, so she turned her attention to the voice of the newscaster.

'Senator Harvey Robinson, Illinois.'

'So what happens now?' Clara asked.

'It's a voice vote, so he will say 'aye' or 'no',' Jackson said, his eyes firmly fixed on the screen.

Clara could see Senator Robinson for the first time: he was younger than she had expected, perhaps fifty years old. He walked to the front of the Senate, and Clara could see no sign of the terrible pressure he must have been feeling at the moment. She could hardly bear to hear what he had to say, and wondered if he knew that, however he voted, he could not save Daniel.

'Aye.' The Senator's voice rang out clear and certain.

Clara let out her held in breath. She couldn't imagine the courage that it had taken to say that small word. To know the weight of that word on his loved ones and himself.

'I can't believe he did it,' Clara whispered.

'Courage comes in many forms,' Jackson said.

'So does idiocy,' Beth sneered.

'What difference does it make to you?' Clara asked contemptuously. 'You're only interested in the money, and you get that whichever way he voted.'

'It's always so nice to see a man putting his career before family.'

Clara could feel herself tense with anger, and Jackson squeezed her hand. That comment had been aimed at her, she knew. 'Well, a career and devotion to your country is better than selling out a ten-year-old boy for a few bucks!'

'You keep telling yourself that,' Beth said, cold humour showing on her face. 'Your daddy sold you out just like Daniel's family, putting his precious career before his only child. You never even met the man before a few days ago

— you'd probably have walked past him on the street. Money is the only thing you can really trust; and, let's face it, the only thing you really need.'

Clara shook her head. 'Then I feel sorry for you. What a sad life you are living,' she said.

Beth crossed the kitchen in easy strides and dragged her to her feet. Clara felt herself wrenched from Jackson's side but she didn't care. This woman was a monster and she was going to tell her what she thought without fear.

Beth grabbed a handful of her hair and yanked her head back.

'Shut your mouth. You know nothing,' Beth hissed.

Clara marvelled that such a simple statement could raise such ire in her captor, and saw her chance. If she could distract Beth, and maybe even Hollingsworth, then perhaps Jackson's plan, whatever it was, would have more chance of success.

'Did your daddy not love you?' Clara said, letting sarcasm fill every part of her. 'Ah, did he leave you all alone to fend for yourself?' She let every hurtful, hateful thought out. She was lifted off her feet as Beth yanked her against the wall. Clara braced herself but still her head rebounded harshly off of the wall and for a moment she saw stars.

'Seems I struck a nerve,' Clara said forcing herself to smile at Beth's discomfort, ignoring the guilt she felt at inflicting pain, even on someone like Beth.

'You know nothing,' Beth spat through clenched teeth. 'You seem to have forgotten that I'm in charge here and I can make you suffer.' Beth lifted her arm and pressed it so tightly to Clara's throat that she could not have said any more even if she wanted to.

'Actually, I am,' Hollingsworth said as he stepped in besides Beth. 'Let her go.'

Clara wasn't sure what happened next as she fought desperately to get air into her lungs. Stars appeared before her eyes and there was a rushing sound in her ears before everything went dark.

28

The darkness receded and Clara fought to put all the noise and movement into some form of context. She knew where she was, but she had no idea what had happened. She rolled onto her side and lifted herself up on her elbow, searching for signs of Jackson. A crash drew her attention, and she watched in horror as Jackson flew through the air and landed hard by the back door. She forced herself up on to her knees, desperate to be by his side, to check that he was . . . She forced the thought away.

Beth stumbled to her feet, her lip bleeding from where someone or something had struck her.

'That hurt,' she said reproachfully to Hollingsworth who was standing to one side.

'Then you should do as you're told.' Hollingsworth's manner was bored and uninterested.

'You couldn't have done this without me,' Beth said. 'I'm the reason that you have the boy in the first place.'

Hollingsworth ignored her and walked towards Jackson's crumpled body. He let out a sharp kick. Jackson's body moved, but there were no signs of life. Clara bit back a sob; all eyes were away from her, and she knew that this was her chance. She had to take it; not for herself — she wasn't sure if she cared what happened to her now — but for Daniel.

'Don't you dare walk away from me!' Beth's scream seemed to roll around the kitchen. Her focus was entirely on Hollingsworth; and so, without standing, Clara slid on her knees towards the door that led to the rest of the house. She tried to keep her movements as noiseless as Jackson always managed, but the scraping of her jeans on the tiled floor seemed loud in her ears, and she was certain at any moment she would be noticed.

'Stop!' Clara froze at the words and

the unmistakable sound of the safety of a gun being clicked off. She forced herself to turn around — if this was it, they were going to have to shoot her face-to-face.

A single gunshot rang out and Clara tensed. There was no pain, which surprised her, but then she wondered if a person had time to react to a serious wound. The moment passed and there was still nothing — no pain, no burning, nothing. Nothing but the noise of a struggle. Looking back around the island in the centre of the kitchen, she could see Beth and Hollingsworth fighting for the gun. Neither of them was injured, and Clara could make out shattered glass from the kitchen window.

Forcing her body to respond, she found her feet and fled out of the kitchen door, knowing that at any moment one of them would win the fight and come for her. She skidded to a halt outside the room at the front of the house and a memory resurfaced. Daniel had spoken of another man, kinder than Grotbags so unlikely to be Hollingsworth, but none-theless involved in this whole mess. She paused, wondering if he was inside the room with Daniel. Should she wait? One of the neighbours was bound to have called the police by now, having heard the gunshot. Surely they would be here soon.

A further bang from the kitchen galvanised her into action. There was no time to wait; she would have to risk it. She put her hand to the door and tried the handle, cursing when she remembered that Beth had locked it. She looked around for something she could jimmy the door with, and then remembered what she had seen in the basement. Not worrying about making noise now, she ran down the stairs into the darkness.

The metal felt heavy in her hand, and she felt more confident now that she had something she could use as a weapon. She wedged the metal end of the spade into the door jamb and tried to force it open. The wood squealed but didn't give at all. She wanted to shout out to Daniel to stand away from the door, to keep him safe, but the sounds from the kitchen had gone and she felt sure her disappearance was about to be discovered. She tried to wedge the door open again, but nothing happened. Running her hand over the door, the wood felt less solid. She took one look at the spade in her hand, heaved it back over her shoulder, and let it swing at the middle of the door. Her efforts were rewarded as the outer layer spilt. She swung the spade back again and again, and finally she could see through into the room beyond. She dropped the spade and used her plastered arm to lever out sections of the door.

'Daniel? It's Clara, are you there?' There was no sound or movement from inside the room, and the fear that Beth or Hollingsworth had already carried out their threat filled her. Ignoring the splintered wood cutting into her good hand, she grabbed a jagged edge and pulled. Finally it came away and she fell backwards onto the floor. She launched herself forward and squeezed through the gap in the door, her top ripping on a splintered plank. She ignored the pain as the wood dug into her side.

She searched the room frantically for signs of Daniel, and her eyes settled on a small figure curled into a ball on the sofa at the far end of the room. Clara let out a moan of fear and rushed to his side.

'Daniel? Can you hear me?' She could feel the tears start to race down her cheeks as she gently shook the still form. She could find no obvious injuries, and Daniel stirred under her touch.

'Daniel?' she asked again. He murmured something that she couldn't make out. She scanned the room and noticed a medicine bottle on the coffee table. Lifting it up to the light, she could see it was almost empty, but had once contained night-time cough relief. Daniel had obviously been drugged. She returned to the sofa and bent down, lifting the boy in her arms. The weight on her broken arm sent sharp stabbing pains up to her shoulder, but she pushed the sensation aside and focused on moving towards the door. There was no key on this side and the door refused to budge, the lock obviously stronger than the door itself. She lay Daniel gently on the floor and tried the window. This was locked too, and there was no sign of a key.

Fighting down a howl of frustration, she turned her attention back to the door. Grabbing a throw from the sofa, she laid it on the floor and gently lifted Daniel on to it. Making her way back to the door, she checked that the hall was empty and then squeezed back through the hole she had made. She reached back through, grabbed a corner of the throw and pulled the unconscious Daniel towards her. Once he was close enough, she pushed both hands through the hole, wrapped the throw around Daniel to protect him from the jagged edges of the door, and pulled him towards her.

The glass in the front door shattered, and Clara had just enough time to haul Daniel into her arms and protect his face when a green cylinder rolled to her feet. She hugged Daniel to her tightly, and tried to fight the fire in her throat and the burning pain in her arm. She could just make out shouts and the sounds of heavy-booted footfalls, when someone tried to pull Daniel from her grip.

She tightened her arms and turned her body away. She was dimly aware of a muffled sound, like someone trying to talk to her from far away, but she had no idea if the owner of the arms was friend or foe. She wasn't going to give Daniel to anyone she didn't trust, and right now that was everyone. The grip shifted and she felt herself lifted into the air. She clung to Daniel and whispered to him that everything was going to be all right, even though she had no idea if this was true or not.

A few steps, and Clara found herself outside. The air seemed to cool the burning in her throat, and although her eyes still streamed, she could now make out the road, full of cars and emergency vehicles, from which blue and red lights flashed and whirled. The man carrying her was dressed all in black. He wore a black helmet and a mask covered his face. It should have seemed sinister, Clara thought, but his presence was comforting, as she felt sure that he was one of the good guys. She was gently lowered onto a stretcher at the back of one of the ambulances and the man strode away.

'Miss Radley? My name is Lyn; I'm a paramedic. Would you mind if I check out young Daniel here?' Her voice was gentle and her face smiling. Clara tried to obey, tried to loosen her grip, but she couldn't. She looked down at her arms, willing them to let go.

'They gave him cough medicine, to make him sleep, I think. I'm not sure how much they gave him.'

'That's really helpful, Clara, thank you,' Lyn said as she lifted Daniel from her arms. She turned and laid him gently on a nearby stretcher as if knowing that Clara could not bear to let him out of her sight. Clara watched as the paramedic swiftly went about checking on the boy's well-being. She felt a blood-pressure cuff wrap around her arm, and looked up to see another paramedic, who had been assigned to her care.

'There are no obvious injuries, Clara. Daniel is going to be fine, but we are going to take you both to the hospital to get you checked over. It might be a while before Daniel wakes up, but there shouldn't be any lasting ill-effects from the medicine.'

A car drew up and a young couple got out. A man in a black suit stepped out from the front seat and gestured in Clara's direction. The couple ran forward, and in an instant Clara knew that these were Daniel's parents.

'Is he all right? Did they hurt him?' Daniel's father asked as his wife swept her son into her arms.

'Daniel seems fine, Mr Robinson,' Lyn said calmly, placing a gentle hand on the boy's head. 'His captors appear to have given him some cough medicine to make him sleepy, but the effects should wear off with time.'

Knowing that Daniel was safely back with his parents made the emptiness inside Clara grow. She no longer had Daniel to focus on, and she knew she would now have to let the grief out. Jackson was gone. She had known him less than two weeks, but couldn't imagine her life without him. She wasn't sure what she would do, but knew she needed to see him one more time, to say goodbye and to finish the conversation.

She pulled at the blood-pressure cuff and felt the Velcro give. The paramedic who had been standing beside her was in the back of the ambulance fetching supplies. Clara slid off the stretcher and made her way through the maze of cars. She had seen enough cop shows on TV to know that Jackson would have been left where he fell, until the medical examiner was happy for the body to be removed.

Clara swallowed the lump in her throat as she marvelled at the calm manner in which her mind was processing the information. Jackson was gone; he would be treated as evidence of this terrible crime, photographed and measured and then bundled into a black bag. She knew at the moment she couldn't let that happen, and she started to run. She had to stop them. She had to make them see that he was a person, a brave man who had sacrificed himself for her and for a small boy.

29

The house and garden were surrounded by yellow police tape, officers in uniform, and men and women in sharp suits who walked around purposefully. No one seemed to pay Clara any attention. She forced herself to slow her pace, knowing that running would only draw attention to herself. She fell into step with a man and woman wearing FBI windbreakers, and passed through the front door unnoticed. The pair stepped into the front room where Daniel had been held, and Clara moved on towards the kitchen.

The door had been propped open and there were yellow evidence triangles everywhere. People in white suits knelt here and there, taking photographs and measurements. Around the outside edge of the kitchen, away from the evidence, stood more FBI agents taking notes and discussing points quietly. Clara stood to one side of the doorway and tried to calm herself. Two figures lay on the floor: the nearest one was uncovered, and Clara could make out clearly that it was Beth. A pool of blood lay still by her right side, and Clara swallowed the bile that had risen in her throat. It was clear now that Hollingsworth had won the fight for the gun.

Clara tried to process this information. She didn't feel anything at all, not even relief. Beth was dead; it just seemed like a fact that you might read in a history book which had no impact on the present. She guessed it was the shock of everything that had happened and forced herself to look at the body lying at the far end of the kitchen, the place she had last seen Jackson. She bit down the cry in her throat and walked towards him. She knew she would be noticed any moment. She knelt down and reached out a hand to pull back the black sheeting.

'Miss Radley, don't.' A voice sounded behind her and she felt herself gently helped to her feet. 'Miss Radley, what are you doing here? You should be at the hospital.'

At that moment there was a buzz of activity as every agent in the room placed a finger to their ear.

'It's OK, I have her.' The man holding her spoke out loud, but Clara knew he wasn't talking to her.

'Please come with me. You shouldn't be here.' Clara turned slightly and looked into the face of an older man. He smiled gently at her.

'You've just made about fifty FBI agents panic, and that's not easily done, you know.' His smile broadened slightly at her confused face. 'We only just found you, and I don't think anyone was that keen on having to tell the General that we had managed to lose you again.'

'He's here?' Clara asked, and possibly for the first time in her adult life she felt desperate to see him.

'I'll take you to him. He's in the tactical support vehicle, dealing with a few loose ends, but he wants to see you.'

Clara nodded, wondering if that was true. Did he really want to see her? Or was he just checking in, like he would on any soldier under his command? She knew that this was going to be a make-or-break moment. She needed him now, for the first time in her life, and she wasn't sure if she could cope with rejection along with everything else.

Clara let herself be led outside, aware that she was being watched, and wondering for a moment what she must look like. One arm in plaster, faded bruises all over her face, and clothes torn and dirty. She wondered if any of the other agents had known Jackson, if they had been friends, and if they blamed her for his death. Whichever way she looked at it, Jackson was dead because of her, and she didn't think she would ever be able to shift that last memory of him lying still and crumpled in the corner.

The agent knocked on the door to a large van and it was opened.

'Can you give us the room?' a voice sounded, and Clara was sure it was the General's. Two men in military uniform and a woman in a suit walked down the steps, each nodding to her as they passed. Clara put a foot on the first step and felt almost paralysed, but she forced herself to step up and into the room. Inside, there were banks of computers and equipment, but Clara's eyes sought out the person in the room. He stood straight-backed, but Clara thought she could detect some tension in his hands, and for a fleeting moment she thought he was nervous. She didn't know what to say, so for once said nothing.

The General swallowed, then took the distance between them in easy strides, and for the first time in her life she felt herself embraced by her father.

'I'm so sorry, Clara,' he said.

To her surprise, in that moment Clara was able to let go of all the resentment and anger and hug him back, feeling safe.

'I never wanted this for you or your mother.'

Clara pulled away. 'Mum!' she yelped. 'I have to call her, she must be frantic!'

Two hands steadied her.

'I called your mother as soon as I knew you were safe and secure.'

Clara blinked, somehow surprised that that had been his priority.

'I know what you must think of me, Clara, but I care for your mother very much, and I know how hard this time has been on her. It was all I could do to make her stay in the UK where she was safe. She kept threatening to get on a plane. She always was a feisty one.' He smiled now, and Clara could see the affection of a past love.

'And if you were wondering, she is already on the way to the airport. That was the deal. She should be here in about twelve hours.'

The thought of finally seeing her mum and maybe the rest of her family brought the emotions forward and she let out a sob. She found herself pulled into her father's arms again and he kissed her gently on her head.

'It's OK, Clara, everything is going to be OK.'

But Clara knew that wasn't true. Jackson, the first man she had ever truly loved, was gone forever. She had kept so much clamped down inside her, and now she let it out, clutching onto her father's uniform and letting him hold her.

'We need to get you checked out at the hospital, and I can get a progress report on my men.'

The words made Clara's latest sob subside.

'People were hurt?' she asked, wondering who else had been injured because of her. She pulled back so she could see her father's face and its puzzlement.

'Agent Henry was injured. I understood you were with him at the time?'

Clara felt the colour drain from her

face and the all-too-familiar ringing in her ears. Hands forced her to sit in a chair.

'Clara?' The General's voice was full of concern — and, if she didn't know better, a touch of panic. He was kneeling beside her, his hands on hers.

'He died,' was all she could whisper.

'No, Clara. He is in surgery, and it's serious, but initial reports are that he should make a full recovery with time.'

'Then who? Who was in the kitchen?'

The General had a look of sudden understanding.

'The body was that of former Agent Hollingsworth. He was killed by one of my agents, an inside man.'

Clara started to cry again. She wondered if it was a dream, that she wanted it to be true so badly that she was imagining this whole conversation. So much of the last few weeks had been surreal.

'Let's get you to the hospital and we can get an update.'

The General led Clara outside and

towards a black SUV. A young Army officer stood to attention.

'Hospital, Jenson.'

'Yes, sir.' The back door was opened and Clara slid in, but before the General could step in beside her, he was stopped.

'General, we need you to take a look at these after-action reports.'

'It will have to wait, Agent Townsend. I need to take my daughter to the hospital to get checked out. Webster can review it for now and update me later.'

'Yes, sir.'

The General slid into the seat beside Clara, and she looked at him, really looked at him, for the first time.

'Thank you,' she said.

'I've made mistakes, Clara, but please believe me that at the time I thought they were for the best. I would like the opportunity to get to know you now, if you would be willing to consider it.'

There had been many times in the past when Clara had rehearsed what she would say to her absent father if he ever appeared in her life. Most of them involved her telling him where to go, explaining in great detail that he had removed himself from her life and she had no room for him. But something had changed. Imaginary conversations were one thing, but to say that to someone standing in front of you asking for another chance was an entirely different matter. Deep down, Clara knew there was more to it. She trusted Jackson. He knew her father better than she did, and his faith was unwavering. Jackson's belief that the General was a good man would not falter, and so Clara knew that she would give him the chance. They could not go back, he could not be her dad . . . but perhaps they could find a new way. Clara reached over and squeezed his hand.

'I have a dad,' she said carefully. The General nodded, his face neutral, but even after knowing him for such a short time, Clara thought she could detect a glimmer of pain and regret.

'I know, Clara. I'm not trying to take

his place, but I would like the opportunity to get to know you. Perhaps we can find a way to have some sort of relationship.'

'I'd like that,' Clara said, feeling suddenly shy and turning to look out of the window.

30

Clara tried to stay seated, but all she could do was pace up and down. The lights in the intensive care unit had been dimmed to indicate the late hour, but the activity remained constant. The General had spoken to the doctors and she had a clean bill of health, apart from her broken arm and fading bruises. Jackson's condition was critical but stable, and all they could do now was wait. The General had offered to wait with her, but Clara had seen from the phone calls and other interruptions that he was needed elsewhere, so she had sent him away with a promise to call his private line if she needed anything. If the General suspected that she and Jackson had formed some kind of relationship in their short time together, he offered no comment, but seemed to accept her need to stay by his side. Her family would be arriving in the morning, and transport had been arranged to bring them straight to the hospital.

A nurse stepped in and checked on the various machines before writing on the board at the bed's end.

'Can I get you anything?' she asked with a smile. 'Some coffee or something to eat?' Clara shook her head.

'I can fix up a cot for you. You should try to get some sleep. The doctor doesn't expect Agent Henry to wake for several hours yet, and it may be longer.'

'I'm fine, really. I don't think I could sleep, but if I do get tired I can use the chair.' As if to reassure the nurse, Clara moved to sit in the chair beside the bed, and reached out for Jackson's hand. The nurse studied her for a moment.

'Just press the call bell if you need anything.'

Clara watched as the nurse left the room.

'You should get some sleep,' a voice murmured, and Clara nearly jumped out of her skin. Her eyes flashed back to Jackson's face, which was smooth with apparent sleep. Clara leaned forward.

'Jackson?' she asked quietly, sure she was hearing things, or that maybe the lack of sleep was making her delusional.

'Did you think it was the ghost of patients past speaking?' he said, his voice hoarse, before slowly opening his eyes.

'You scared me,' was all Clara could say, with a hand to her chest. Then, as she remembered where they were and why: 'Should I get the nurse? Does it hurt?' The last question made her want to slap her forehead; it seemed even the events of the last few weeks could not cure her of the foot-in-mouth syndrome that she seemed to suffer from.

'No nurses, all they want to do is stick you with needles.' Jackson closed his eyes.

'You got stabbed, and you're worried about an injection?' Clara was incredulous now, but the wry smile on Jackson's face told her that he was, as usual, teasing her. Clara fought the urge to punch him in the arm, thinking that right now it was probably not a good plan.

'Are you OK?' Jackson turned his head towards her and opened his eyes again. It seemed to take quite a bit of effort, and she put her hand on his arm to reassure him.

'I'm fine; why are you always worried about me? You're the one lying in a hospital bed.'

'You're the kind of person that people worry about.' His eyes were shut again now and he sounded as if he was drifting off.

'Always getting other people in to trouble, that's me,' she said softly.

'That's not it,' he said with a sleepy sigh. 'You're special, Clara, and that's why I want to keep you safe, now and always.'

Clara blinked, not certain that she had really heard those words.

'Morphine loosens the tongue of even the most taciturn man.' Clara turned; the nurse was back, and she gave Clara a knowing look. 'He'll probably sleep some more. I'll rouse you if he wakes up,' she promised, handing Clara a hospital blanket.

Clara tried to sleep, to empty her mind, but sleep was like a distant memory. *It was over*, she told herself firmly, *she was safe* — but she knew deep down that fear was not the reason she couldn't sleep. She wanted — no, *needed* — to talk to Jackson. She needed to know where she stood, how he felt about her. The morning would bring her family, and although she was desperate to see them, she knew that a private conversation with Jackson after that point would be near-impossible. She would be commandeered by her family, and Jackson would be in hospital and then would slowly slip away from her, out of her life.

Of course, she knew that it was possible that he felt nothing real for her. Danger was a great aphrodisiac, and she couldn't blame him if, in the cold light of day, he realised it was all a big mistake. Agent Summers' words also rang in her ears, but she pushed them aside. He was a traitor and a terrible person, which meant his opinion was worth less than nothing. She shifted in the chair, having refused to have a cot set up.

'Will you settle down? Some of us are trying to sleep here.'

Clara looked up and realised that Jackson was looking at her; his eyes seemed clearer and his gaze steadier.

'Sorry,' she said softly. 'Go back to sleep.'

'I will if you will.'

'I'm trying. It's like I'm too tired to sleep . . . is that even possible?'

'Common after what you've been through; but you're safe now, Clara. This place is crawling with police and the FBI; no one is going to get near you, trust me.'

Clara was silent; she knew that now was her chance, but wasn't sure she could get the words out.

'Yeah, that's not it, though.' She kept her gaze firmly fixed on his face and was sure she could detect a slight eyeroll. He let out a long-suffering sigh, and then moved slightly so that he could see her more clearly. Clara watched as he winced in pain and wondered if now was really a good time.

'Out with it, then. Neither of us are going to get much sleep until you've said what you need to say.'

Clara swallowed, and tried to formulate her thoughts and feelings into something close to coherent.

'OK.' She took a deep breath and looked at him again to make sure he was still awake.

'I'm listening, Clara. It's two a.m., and I'm recovering from a stab wound, but I'm still listening.'

It was Clara's turn to roll her eyes as he grinned slightly.

'The thing is, I'm not sure what this — ' She waved her hand between him and her. ' — means to you . . . but it means a lot to me. And I know what you are going to say. We shouldn't have, I have no business falling in love with you, and I have no idea how you feel. You said that we shouldn't, and then we did, and maybe you don't feel anything but protective towards me, and I get it if that is all you feel, and that's even OK, but I need to tell you how I feel . . . ' Clara stopped when she felt his hand rest on hers.

'I'm on morphine here and I'm not sure I can keep up with you. Can you summarise for me, sweetcheeks?'

Clara had no idea how to summarise what she was feeling. She wasn't even sure *she* knew how she felt, really.

'I love you.' Clara blinked in surprise as she realised that they had been her words. It was like her body had gone into automatic pilot and just said it, bypassing her brain and tendency to procrastinate.

'Clara . . . ' Jackson started, and Clara braced herself for the inevitable rejection that was to follow. She felt like a balloon that had been pierced by a drawing pin. She looked down at her hands, unable to make eye contact with him, not wanting to see the sympathy or embarrassment or any other emotion Jackson might be feeling.

'Relationships form in the field, and they feel very real at the time — but that doesn't mean they *are*, or that they are in everyone's best interest.'

'I knew you would say that,' she said quietly. 'You may not believe me, you might think it's still the shock or something, but I know how I feel and I've never felt this way before.' She looked up now and held his gaze.

'You've never been in a life-or-death situation before.' His words were gentle, but Clara got the distinct impression she was being handled.

'Yes, I have, actually. I've worked for aid agencies in the worst places in the world, and I've seen and experienced more than you think.'

'It wasn't meant as an insult.'

'I know that,' she said a little crossly.

'I'm just saying that I know what you mean about dangerous situations, but I'm telling you this is different. How I feel for you is separate to that.' She frowned now, wishing she could make him understand.

'Let's say for a moment that what you said is true, and that our situation had nothing to do with it — but then what? I'm a Federal Agent and I work in the US; you're studying for your PhD in the UK. How would that work?'

'We'd make it work, if we wanted to. Do you want to?' She stared at him, trying to read his thoughts. Jackson said nothing, and she wondered if she would become just another woman in his past.

'Well, we could start with how you feel ... about me.' She could feel herself blush.

'I'm not sure it matters how I feel.'

'It matters to me,' Clara said.

'Well, against my better judgement, I care about you, I love you, but I'm not sure it changes anything.' He turned his head and stared at the ceiling.

Jackson felt like his mind and heart would explode at any moment. He loved her, he knew that. Deep down, he knew that he had never felt like this before, he had never loved someone as he loved Clara. But his mind was never one to avoid the facts. He was a serial 'love 'em and leave 'em' type. He didn't know if he was capable of a long-term relationship, and after protecting her from everyone else, he was sure as hell not going to hurt her himself.

'It changes everything,' Clara said softly. She watched his face closely.

'I'm not good at this, Clara. I'm terrible at relationships, I've never had a successful long-term relationship, and however hard I try, I will hurt you.' He made himself say the words out loud. He knew he had to tell her the truth. This was who he was, and he wasn't sure he would be able to change, however much he wanted to.

'No, you won't,' she said.

'You don't know that.' He stared at her. Her absolute faith in him amazed him, and somehow he could feel a part of himself wonder if she was right — that he could love her, be with her. And he promised himself in that moment that he would do whatever it took to love her and protect her.

'Yes, I do.' She stood up and brushed a gentle kiss on his cheek, watching him closely all the while. Her eyes fixed on his and she leaned in to kiss him properly. She felt him respond in kind and an arm wrap around her. When they finally parted, she felt breathless and light-headed.

'You are literally killing me here,' he whispered but knowing that he would take her kisses and the pain over anything else in the world.

'Sorry,' she said, but her tone told him that she wasn't really. 'Face it: I love you Jackson Henry, and I'm not going anywhere.'

'What about . . . '

Clara put her fingers to his lips to stop him finishing his sentence. His mind started to buzz with all the issues y would face. His job, her studies, e fact that they lived thousands of iles apart . . .

'We can work out all the practical sues later, Agent, but for right now, all hat matters is I want you and you want me.'

He shook his head. 'There'll be trouble ahead, you know.' He knew there would be, but he didn't care. Clara was too important, too special, and he had made up his mind. He wasn't about to let her go, whatever it cost him.

Clara smiled. 'I know.' She eased herself onto the edge of the bed. 'And I'm kind of looking forward to it.'

With some effort, Jackson moved to make room, and Clara gently curled alongside him. He kissed her on the head.

'I love you, Clara Radley.'

'I love you too, Jackson Henry.'

★   ★   ★

Clara sighed, feeling like the last th[e] weeks had been the best and worst [of] her life. If you had told her before t[he] night that she would be curled [up] beside an American Special Agent i[n a] military hospital, having been on t[he] run, afraid for her life, she would hav[e] fallen off her chair laughing. Yet here she was. Her life could not have undergone a bigger change, but she knew that she loved this man with all of her heart, and nothing would ever change that.

'Now, can we finally get some sleep? Some of us need it.'

Clara laughed softly and snuggled in tightly before closing her eyes and allowing sleep to take her. Now all she had to do was explain this to her family!